DEEP SEA PREDATOR

By Brian Gatto

DEEP SEA PREDATOR

WWW.SEVEREDPRESS.COM

ISBN: 978-1-923165-65-6

FOR MATT TAYLOR

Thank you for the tour.

A DEDICATION TO *JAWS*

The five decades the film has impacted will be felt for more to come.

CHAPTER ONE

A job by the sea.

Kane Grant was not what one would call a prestigious personality. His self-esteem wore out years ago. There was no motivation left. The drive he once had left him in the dust like his son. His wife, dead and buried on their home property. Family? What was that to him. He had nothing left. Nothing, except a preserve to tend to. It was a gig he had inherited from his nephew. He thought it would do him good.

He could remember the conversation as if it were yesterday. Kane had been a regular bum with nothing to do. No one to care for or live for. Nothing to do. His nephew, God bless his soul, had given it all to get him into the business of maintenance to what was essentially a tourist attraction. He had used words like *Change* and *Happiness*. Thankfully, it was not a sham nor a crazed illusion. He was more in tune with Farm Pond than he was at his own place. That was until the tourist season came around.

Even when there was nothing left, life still seemed to burden him. To kick him while he was down.

Today was no different. As he strode down the grassy pathway, he tried to find peace. The property was one of natural unification. Seagulls could be seen scouring the surface in the shallow portions of the preserve. They looked for mussels and tiny crabs to peck at until satisfied they were up for consumption. It was early morning, approximately 4:30.

The rooster, a gift from his sister, would be up and squawking soon. He hated that damned thing with the same passion it probably felt for him. He always swore it possessed his sister's disdain for everything and everyone. She married a bread winner a long time ago. Back when she was halfway normal. It was not long until she slipped back into her ways. Her true colors were as red as her anger.

He focused on the first stop up ahead. The faded red shed was the most rustic spot on the property. It still held up well, withstanding all sorts of weather. He made a mental note to give it a paint over this summer.

Ugh. The thought of this summer was what brought him back to his brooding self. Sure, tourism was good for the island of Martha's Vineyard. Still, it did not ease his annoyance or lower his blood pressure. Flocks of them, all flaunting their apparel with logos and drawings, marched onto the island off the ferry every year. This year was different though.

"Fifty goddamned years," he mumbled.

He had only seen the film once. It was a good ol' fisherman's adventure tale. Calling it a classic was a bit of a stretch, he thought. Besides, he was a land-lover. He did not need complications of running a boat on top of everything else he had to do. So, he saw *Jaws* as more of a natural comedy than a straight adventure thriller.

A trial and error on his part was that he argued with the town on these fans. He fought tooth and nail to get the ferries to bring less people. They took note, so they claimed. Whether or not anything was to be done about it was yet to be seen. That was in February after all. Valentine's Day celebrations were in talk during that time.

The whole island had turned into a festive fabrication. They served shark-themed punch and held photo ops with faux fish dangling around during the summer of love. It was all nonsense. The movie was older than most of its current fans.

Now it was the middle of June. He had not been in town for a couple of weeks. Last time he was, he noticed the abundance of tourists. There seemed to be more during that time than the 49th anniversary of the film. It was getting ridiculous. All he wanted to do was get some paint for the shed. What would be a near hour trip turned into two and a half with the traffic.

A silver lining was there. He knew he was not the only one done with it all. Sick of the constant vandalism and prick parading around. His neighbor, a fellow by the name of Keith Sturges, shared his disappointment. Times were changing against them.

It might be a good idea to head over there today, Kane thought as he entered the barn.

The warm welcome he was used to seeing was not bestowed to him. Instead, his animals looked nervous, on edge. They kept their heads up as if something was stalking them in the rafters. Then, Kane realized they were sniffing. It sounded like the world's most obnoxious snorer inside. The noise reverberated around, bouncing off the walls and into his ears. Occasional brief grunts and whinnying could be heard but they were smelling in unison no doubt.

"What's gotten into you guys?"

It was not until a faint breeze passed by. It carried with it the stench of earthly odor. Kane immediately covered his nose and mouth with his arm.

He thought back on the dead deer he found yesterday by the pond. "Great. Who died today?"

Speaking to himself always made him feel insane. Though talking to the animals was worse in his opinion. He decided to get it over with quickly and dropped some feed into their buckets that hung from their stalls. After filling the first couple, he realized there was silence. No clumsy chewing could be heard. He turned and saw they remained untouched.

"What the devil?"

One of the horses then let out a wretched neigh and kicked outward with its back legs. The siding buckled slightly and light from the early morning sun could be seen spilling in. Kane was shocked.

"What are you doing? Stop that this instant!"

The horse paid no mind and rose up high. It stood nearly eight feet off the ground before coming back down on the stall door. Kane backed up and out of the way as he saw hinges breaking. The horse then bucked up and down and then plowed through.

"Stop!" He tried to sound calm. It was not easy, nor did it seem to be working.

He continued to back up, tripping over a pail of water on the ground. Stumbling back, he managed to grab onto a support beam and stop himself from falling onto the ground. The horse continued to hop around.

"Sally! Stop!" he cried out.

In response, she let out a wildly loud shriek and galloped towards the entrance. Her only clear exit. There, she was greeted by the warm sight of something that made her change course and charge for the house.

Kane stepped outside. "Get back here!"

He then stopped when he caught a familiar whiff in the air. Following the trail of stench, the source was clearly coming from down by the pond. There, he saw a massive shape. He figured it was just a log. Though, when he squinted, he could make out key details that were not of normality for a part of a tree. It was too smooth, the texture looked like the back of a whale.

"What the? What's an orca doing out here?"

The killer whale was the only one that crossed his mind. It was a similar size and shape after all.

Quickly, he began towards the house. He was thankful Sally did not charge inside and wreck the place. He would have to track her down and get her back in her pen. In the meantime, he walked inside and went for the double barrel shotgun situated right next to the door. He checked the chamber and confirmed it was loaded.

Returning outside, the sun was beginning to fill the sky more. It always amazed him how bright it could get in such a short amount of time outside. With that, he was able to see the animal better. As well as what was next to it.

Step after step, he found himself slowing. Each time he lifted a leg, it was as if there were bricks tied to his shoes. He only picked up the pace when he realized what was on the ground by the pond.

"Keith!" he cried out in alarm.

Soon, he was running. He had not kept this pace in a long while. Being fifty-eight definitely had its effects on his poor old bones. He managed to ignore them, but only for so long. Slowing, he eventually had to stop. He took a few deep breaths, but the smell was abhorrent. Gagging, he nearly expelled his bacon and egg breakfast onto his lawn.

He looked up and saw how close he was. "I'm coming, Keith!"

There were times the man would pull jokes on Kane. Not that they were all that physical, but this here was going beyond what the seventy-four-year-old was capable of. He was soon close enough to fall onto one knee beside his long-time friend.

"Keith. Speak to me! Are you alright?"

"Huh? What?" he responded weakly.

"Oh, thank the lord!"

"Where am I? What time is it?"

"Time to get your sorry ass up."

Keith nodded slowly and began to climb to his feet. He fell back down when he noticed the thing in front of him.

"What the hell is that?" he exclaimed.

Whatever it was, it was facing away from them. It was big. A girthy mass of greyish black skin. There were oddities about its shape.

"One thing is for certain," Kane said, exasperated. "It's no whale."

CHAPTER TWO

To die for.

He had waited for this week all year. A trip up to their favorite site at Camp Evergreen was exactly what Daniel Brightly needed after the work schedule he had been dealt with. The 9-5 work life was hard for most. He would kiss the ground his employer walked on if he were so lucky. His life focused on the routine 24/7 schedule. He was on call and, worst of all, salary.

It was a decision he made that his former boss begged him not to. He wanted to prove himself to the institute but, more importantly, to himself. No longer was he procrastinating on everything. He wanted to take advantage of his life, grab it by the reins and scream at the heavens.

That was two years ago. Now, he was dreading his choice. He was exhausted. Over worked, tired, and just done with it all. Thankfully he accumulated enough time to take off two weeks and still be paid for them. Now he was here with his family.

Little Joseph Brightly was still in his pajamas. They had little sharks on them. He always slept so peacefully, even when he was a baby. A blessing because he could not imagine having a crying infant around when he had to write his thesis papers. He was old enough to have his own tent now. At eight years old, he was very smart and aware of his surroundings for a boy of that age.

Daniel turned and looked over at his wife. Sandra was the epitome of beauty. She was the rare gift from God. Not only did he love her deeply, but his friends and family liked her. At first, his overly strict mother was a thing of caution. *Don't let my mother get to you. She can be picky.*

He had said this right at his parents' doorstep. Whether or not she heard was up for debate because she opened the front door merely seconds after. She was welcoming. Perhaps it was her way of getting back at him for his comment. Part of him wanted to believe that. If she did, she would play the part for over ten years. Well, too. There was never a hint of disdain towards her. She even made a toast at their wedding.

Partly opening her eyes, she looked up at him.

"Good morning, sunshine."

"Hey you." She smiled and stretched.

Looking at her, she could not help but notice.

"You're studying me like one of your fish."

"At least you don't smell like them."

She giggled.

"Mom, Dad?" a small voice called from the tent.

"Yes, Joey?" Sandra said sweetly.

"Can I come out? I've been awake forever."

"Just wait until Mommy and Daddy come out. Okay?" she replied with warmth.

"I have to use the bathroom."

"Alright." Daniel got off the blowup mattress. "I'll be right out."

"Okay," Joseph said while yawning.

Sandra grabbed him around the strap of his boxers as she spoke softly. "You were wonderful last night."

"What can I say," he whispered. "The woods bring out the animal in me."

They had made love twice last night. It would be crude seeing as Joseph was a mere three yards away, but he was always a deep sleeper. He always said he did not snore when he slept. It was the one give away because it was not true. *His nostrils draw in so much air that some of it probably touches his brain,* Daniel had joked once.

Yet, somehow, he's not an airhead, she would chuckle back.

Daniel stepped outside and made his way over to Joseph's tent. Before he could reach the zipper, the door flap swung open, and he hopped out. "I need to go bad!"

"Then let's hurry."

"Why can't we just go over by the bushes?"

"Because then the whole camp will smell," Daniel chuckled. "C'mon now."

He guided him up the hill and towards the facilities.

Much to Daniel and especially Joey's dismay, there was already a line building. Three people were outside while at least two more waited in the building. There was one boy, not much older than Joseph, who was doing a little dance. He clearly had been waiting a while too.

That was one thing he hated about this campsite. Sure, there were plenty of stalls. The problem was, during the summer season, they were either not cleaned entirely or left out of order. Normally the latter.

"Must be hard finding help these days," Daniel whispered under his breath.

"Yep," the guy next to him grumbled. "Everyone wants to make money. When places don't pay enough, even if the job is good, their turnover rate skyrockets."

Daniel turned to see the man was holding the dancing boy's hand. His own looked red.

"Boy's got a tight grip," he chuckled.

"Tighter than my wife's the day he was born. I don't know where he gets it from."

They both shared a momentary laugh.

"Daddy! I have to go now!" the boy whined.

As if to answer his demands, two people walked out of the stalls simultaneously. The two inside then hurried in.

"God, if this keeps up, we're going to be late for the ferry," Daniel stated.

"You guys going to Martha's Vineyard?" the man next to him asked.

"Yes. How did you know?"

"Jaws? It turns fifty in just a few days. People are flocking."

Daniel stared at him blankly.

"You didn't know?"

"I did. I didn't know it was such a big deal though."

"Well, it's going to be the topic of the town, erm, island."

"Oh," Daniel feigned interest.

"Hopefully you have something else to do there. There will probably be a lot of waiting around."

Two more people got out of the stalls. The first outside rushed in. The boy released his grip on his father's hand and ran for the door.

"I'm also going to visit an old friend."

"Oh. Does he do Jaws stuff?"

"No. He's a doctor."

"Are you?"

Daniel sighed. He had been asked this question one too many times these past few weeks. "I guess you could say that."

"Oh." The man's eyebrows rose, interest clearly piqued.

"I specialize in fish." He tried to put it as plainly as possible.

"A marine biologist."

"Almost. I study extinct species."

"If they're extinct, how do you study them?"

Great, we've got a smart ass here, Daniel thought. "Their bones."

"I thought they had that stuff that disappears after a short amount of time?"

"Cartilage? No, that's sharks."

"I see." He paused. "Then how do they know about extinct sharks?"

"Their teeth." Daniel's agitation showed clearly on his face.

"Fascinating. What's the biggest creature you studied?"

Oh boy. I went on vacation just to lecture people on extinct marine reptiles and fish.

"No offense," Daniel paused, waiting for the man to state his name.

"McGrew."

"McGrew," he repeated slowly. "I came out here to spend time away from work."

"Say no more!" McGrew said cheerfully. "I get it. I sell cars. The last thing I'd want is for people to tell me about all the new models released while I'm on vacation."

"Thank you for understanding."

One man walked out of the bathroom. McGrew was about to step forward but turned and looked down at Joey. "Go on. I can wait."

"Thanks, Mister!" He ran inside and quickly into the stall. He did not shut the door.

"Kids," McGrew chuckled.

"Is he your only?"

"Me, nah. I've got more back at the campsite. The wife's just finishing breakfast. We'll be heading out soon. She wants to hit a few thrift stores first."

"Well, see you on the island," Daniel told him.

"Yeah. If not, enjoy your time at Martha's Vineyard," he beamed.

***

Sometimes it was a chore to be the leading doctor on an island. In Anthony Butler's profession, there was little room for grievances. Despite his ever-growing connection with these people, his detachment to death was more apparent than ever before. It got worse every day. Some called him insensitive. His sense of dry British humor did not help with that. He was not immune to agony or despair. There were lines he would not dare cross without shedding a single tear. It would be a bad look for him.

He thought of himself as having thick skin.

Others thought he was a real bastard. So what? He was *the* island doctor. There was not much else in terms of choice besides interns that came and went with the changing weather. That was one thing he could not stand about Martha's Vineyard. The early hours of the morning were always cold, or at least carried a chill with them. It was a better climate than London. That he could be sure of.

At seventy-one, Anthony was active but not spry. Last year he chipped his hip when falling off a horse. It was a miracle he could still walk straight. What's more was he got back on that same horse at the beginning of this year.

Now he carried his stride into the front of the hospital. The doors slid open, and he walked past them. They closed later. He needed to have new doors installed. *Scratch that,* he thought. *Let the mayor pay for that. I'll classify it as an OSHA violation or something. A risk factor.*

He was about to pass the front desk when a familiar voice called to him.

"You who!" the sweet, delicate tone of Ginger Abernathy sung for him.

Anthony stopped and turned. "What's on the agenda?"

"Well, there are no cases to look at. We do have a few appointments coming in the next couple of hours. It looks like it'll be a slow day so far."

He held out his fist and rapped it on the counter. "Knock on wood."

"Oh, the mayor called. He's expecting you to reach out to him before eight o' clock."

"Mmm. PM."

"No, silly. AM."

"Just as I feared." His tone was grave yet held a humorous side.

Continuing down the hall, he found the door that had a gold plate with his name on it attached on the upper center. He realized it was crooked. Upon further inspection, he saw the screw was stripped. "Great. Make that two calls I'll have to make."

He entered his office and made his way around the desk. Sitting on the leather seat, he made a crawling motion with his fingers on the oak surface. It traveled all the way to the rotary phone. If he was anything, it was old school.

After dialing, it rang three times before the gruff voice of William Owen answered. "This is Mayor Owen speaking."

"Hey, Bill. I heard you were trying to reach me."

"Yes. I have a killer migraine."

"Okay?" His voice trailed off. "Take some ibuprofen."

"I did. Five of the cursed things."

"Did you try meditating?"

"What are you, a therapist now?"

"No. Maybe just take some deep breaths."

He heard the heavy inhaling and exhaling of the man on the other end. He was out of shape and clearly not in the best of health if he was suffering headaches this badly that he had to call him first thing.

"How do you feel?"

"Like a whale washed ashore."

"What?"

"Oh, it's nothing. Just got a call about some animal found dead by two workers over at Farm Pond. Apparently, it's as big as a whale."

"Is it a whale?"

"They don't think so. I'll have to call someone from the mainland and get them to take a look."

At first, Anthony did not want to mention the marine biologist coming to visit him today. He was on vacation and probably did not want to be bothered with questions. Still, he felt obligated. Especially if the animal was dead. The carcass might not be there for long.

"I have a friend, a marine biologist. He's coming to the island today to visit and…"

"Wonderful! Send him out to the Grant and Sturges place. Hopefully we can get to the bottom of this!"

"Can do," Anthony said bitterly. "Anything else?"

"Actually, no! My migraine seems to have passed. You're a miracle worker, Doc! I owe you one!" He hung up the phone.

"You're welcome, Mayor."

Turning his attention to his archaic computer, he looked up the files of who he had appointments with today. He felt the itch to call the mayor back. He wanted new doors bad. As did the nurses and paramedics. He shook his head.

"Next time."

CHAPTER THREE

Dedication.

Morgan Tucker stood leaning against the tour van. A fresh paint job had a shine to it he had not seen on the surface of the vehicle in quite some time. The dark blue was accentuated by the dark windows, tinted black. They were almost like one-way mirrors. You could see out, not in. That's how Morgan felt.

With the Jaws tours picking up and groups of people coming to the island in droves, it was becoming quite an attraction. One that was beginning to wear on him. He loved the movie with passion. Going over the history of it was fun at first. Of course, some would try to point out inconsistencies in the stories. He was only human and telling how he was told. Dedicated research was not required for this position. Most had a cheat sheet. He had it all in his head and from rigorous investigating into the inner workings on the motion picture.

Like the windows, he could see out, but not in. His wife saw the physical toll it took on him come every June. He saw it as fatigue. She thought otherwise.

You're pushing yourself too hard and spending too much time on this movie.

He loved his wife, Moreen, dearly. Sometimes she was right though. This time, he figured she was only half so. He was tired. As he continued to lean against the van, he took another sip of his thermos of coffee. He mumbled something under his breath though not even he knew what. People said it was a vocal tick when he did that. It would not be too hard to believe. His father did it all the time.

A gust of refreshing wind blew by. It was getting warmer as the morning wore on. The tour group would be there shortly, though it looked smaller than usual. Two tickets were bought yet the van was full.

Probably still processing, he thought as he looked it over on his phone again.

"We're going to be late!" he heard someone say in the background.

Looking over the app, he hit the refresh button. After waiting for a few seconds, the page came back. Still only two tickets purchased, bus full.

"Is it here?" the voice came again, clearly a young man.

Morgan looked up and saw him. He looked to be early teens. There was another man walking with him. Grandfather probably. Way too old to be his father. *Although, seeing the parents in Jaws,* Morgan thought and chuckled.

"You guys with the Jaws tour?" he called to them.

"Yes, Tucker's tour?" the older man inquired.

"That'd be me."

"Wonderful!"

They came over and the grandfather shook his hand vigorously. He had a strong grip for such an elderly fellow.

"Where you guys coming in from?"

"Pennsylvania."

"Oh, so not too far."

"Not at all."

"I had a friend in Michigan I wanted to come but they weren't able to make it," the boy said.

"Sorry to hear," Morgan stated. "I'm Morgan Tucker. I'll be your guide for today. We're just waiting for a few more guests. It says the buss will be full."

"About that," yhe old man continued. "I sort of bought out the whole bus. My grandson here is a massive Jaws fan. Showed it to 'im when he was three. I wanted him to get the full experience."

Morgan's face lit up. "Well then! Looks like you two get to claim the front seats!"

"Awesome!" the boy cheered.

They made their way to the van and Morgan slid the door open. "What're your names?"

"I'm Buckley, this is my grandson, Devon."

"Nice to meet you two," Morgan said as he helped them inside. He then slid through the door and made his way around to the driver's side. *Today should be an easy day then.*

***

Waking up was the least of Vernon Hackery's worries. It was becoming a pain all in itself. Not the physical kind either. His memories, sweet and innocent, were shrouded with grief and misery years ago. No matter how many people told him it would get better, it never did. He believed time healed all wounds.

Losing one's spouse was tragic. Have them be your best friend on top of that stung like a bee sting to the heart. He awoke feeling as though he needed to catch his breath. It was suffocation without something solid committing the act. It was deeper than that. It was suffering.

Today seemed to hit harder than most. His vision was blurred and mind foggy. It was akin to being knocked on the head but without the pain. He could not remember his name, let alone his occupation. All he could think about was Julie.

It would have been fifteen years since they were married a week ago. The union of love only lasted eight. Seven years, seven days. It all made sense in his mind. Having a mental beating hurt but a second destroyed him. Almost like some force was making him suffer extra for daring to even try to enjoy himself a week later.

Placing his hands on his face, he pulled them down. His eyelids followed suit as he stared ahead in the dimly lit room. He had not changed much since she passed. The only thing added was a flat-screen television given to him by his brother-in-law, and his uniform which now sat on the back of the chair in the corner. Everything else was hers. The dresser where she sat and brushed her beautiful brown hair and put on make-up. She did not need much, just enough to accentuate her joyful eyes and luscious lips. Across from that, on the other side, was a dresser with several pull out drawers. Her clothes still remained folded neatly inside. His were near the top and stuffed within. He was never the tidiest person.

As he swung his legs over the side of the bed, he maneuvered his feet around until they reached his slippers. He slid them on and made his way out into the hallway. The bathroom was opposite their room. He opened the door and reached for the switch. The light caused him to cover his eyes. After they finally adjusted, he walked over towards the mirror.

"I look like shit," he told himself. "It's my day off, and I look like shit."

Scoffing at his very appearance, he turned the faucet on the sink, bent over, and began to splash cool water on his face. It was refreshing, like a shot of adrenaline that had no side effects. He then returned to look in the mirror. Still looking dreadful, he began towards the shower and turned it on. Hot water instantly shot out of the nozzle. Before he could disrobe, he heard his cell phone ring.

"Son of a bitch." He turned the shower off and made his way back into his room. Every time he entered, he could smell her. He took in a whiff and then walked over towards the dresser.

"Why the hell is he calling me on my day off?" he asked.

"Sheriff, this is Mayor Owen," Bill stated as if the lawman had not already known. "I need you to head out to Grant's farm. He said there's something he needs to show you."

"Call in Rosenthal."

"He's already out trying to control the crowds with the other deputies."

"I have five others. I'm sure one can handle this."

"I tried, no dice."

Sure you did, he thought. He knew full well that the mayor had put in barely any effort to reach a deputy. If any at all. "Tell him I'll be there in half and hour."

"I already did."

He heard a click and sighed. "So much for an easy day."

***

"Seaweed?"

Burt Groves was seated in the fighting chair with his smile quickly fading. He had been fighting what he presumed was a massive fish, a marlin perhaps. Maneuvering with a grace only an old-timely fisherman could achieve, he fought the supposed catch for nearly half an hour.

Standing beside him was his first, and only, mate Stanley Reed. He continued to motion around him and the chair with a cup of water in hand. It never took off, never fought back. The first indications that something was wrong. Now, as they stared at the clump, a feeling of doubt washed over them.

"These catches been getting smaller and smaller, aye Cap?" Stanley stated.

"Must be a big predator around. Orca perhaps," Burt continued. "Dolphin perhaps. Fuckin' whales never know when to mind their own territory. They always have to migrate somewhere else."

"Well, it is their ocean."

"Ha!" Burt spat chewing tobacco into his Styrofoam cup. "It's as much their ocean as the land is ours."

Looking out over the deck at the seaweed, Stanley thought the mess of the barnacle and weed looked odd.

"Is there anything that we can catch out here?" Burt shouted.

"No," Stanley said bluntly.

"That's reassuring."

"Maybe there is something we can salvage though?" Stanley pointed out.

Burt looked at the entanglement and noticed it too. There was something shining within. It glistened under the harsh summer sun. He reached out and grabbed hold, shaking it loose.

"What is it?" Stanley asked.

"It… It looks like a can."

"Goddamnit."

With it now in hand, Burt held it closer. It was just that. A Pabst Blue Ribbon.

"Shit beer, too." He was about to toss it overboard.

"Wait!" Stanley snatched his arm below the elbow. "What's that?"

Bringing it back to them, they noticed it was open on the bottom. Inside there were several flickering lights. They appeared to be switching from green to orange as if turning on and off.

"What the hell?" Burt mumbled.

"Let's take it with us."

"The hell with that. It's probably some government shit. I'm not getting into any more trouble."

"But…" Stanley started.

"…But nothing. I'm not losing Early Bird here!" Burt said, referring to the heap they were currently floating on.

"We might be able to make some money off it. Let it be someone else's problem?" Stanley suggested.

"Fat chance!" Burt whipped the beer can over the side. "We probably wouldn't even make it back to shore with that thing."

"If you say so, Cap."

"I do. Now, take us ashore. I want to freshen up before we go out tonight."

"Got a date?" Stanley asked, surprised.

"Nope. But I have a feeling our luck is about to turn around."

CHAPTER FOUR

Rational fear.

Joseph Brightly had hardly been able to contain himself the whole ride over. The prospect of visiting the island where his favorite movie had been filmed seemed like a dream come true. An astronomical achievement in his mind. While his other friends were visiting Universal Studios, going on all those scary rides and visiting those attractions, he was experiencing the culture of an area that had once embraced the film that put them on the map.

He had done research on the making of Jaws since he was six. Having seen the film at four years old, he had memorized every line and scene verbatim. Now he was interested in its complicated history. The trials and errors associated with the film made for a grueling experience. It was a wonder how the film came out as good as it did.

Smiling wide, Joseph turned his attention from his vintage Jaws Log and looked at his father. He drove with a purposeful expression. It made Joseph think that he was proud that he had such a knowledgeable son, and, in that, it warmed his own heart. He then turned to his mom who seemed a bit distant but willing to start a conversation. Joseph knew she was not an avid fan of Jaws like he and his father were. Still, he appreciated that she came along.

"I think this is the harbor up here," Daniel stated.

"Yeah," Sandra confirmed.

They were currently in Nantucket. The island was but a mere half an hour boat ride away. Joseph's restless legs began to swing back and forth.

"Do you see the boat?" he asked.

"I do. It's over there," Daniel pointed.

Joseph strained his neck and then saw two boats. Both were large vessels with upper and lower decks.

"I've never seen boats that big!"

"They make them bigger," Daniel chuckled.

"Which one are we going on?"

"Uh, not sure, buddy. We'll know soon."

Their vehicle pulled into the parking lot. It was positively packed. Thankfully, ushers were there to assign parking spots. Daniel paid the toll man, and he gave them a ticket to put on the dashboard in return. As they made their way into their little nook, crammed between two other cars, Joseph reached for the door handle.

"Wait, honey," Sandra said sternly. "Let your dad let you out."

"Aw, Mom," he sighed.

Daniel looked around for anything he may have needed. Besides his wallet, hat, and sunglasses, he figured he was all set. He got out and made his way around their car. Joseph practically burst out as he wrapped his arms around his father.

"Thank you!"

"You're welcome, buddy."

He then opened the door for Sandra. "My dear."

She giggled and took his extended hand. Grabbing her purse as he helped her out, she turned and looked back. Nothing else was needed.

"Alright. Lock 'er up." She shut the door and listened for the mechanism to click.

Once it did, they made their way towards the line that was already building. There were several people in one and even more in the other.

"Hopefully they'll be boarding us soon," Sandra wondered.

"Wait!" Joseph shouted. "My book!"

"Don't worry, son. You're an encyclopedia of knowledge on the subject. I don't think you'll need it," Daniel reassured him.

Joseph pouted. "I guess you're right."

It was a while after that the line started to move. As they neared the ferry, Joseph began to show signs of unease. Daniel looked at his son as the boy stared into the water. He would occasionally look at the boat and then back down to the gap between it and the platform.

"Everything alright?" He gave him a gentle nudge.

He did not react well, spinning around and shoving him away a few inches.

"Whoa. Buddy. Are you alright?"

"How do we board the boat? I can't jump far, you know that!"

Sandra placed a tentative hand on his shoulder and pointed. Her son followed the direction her finger aimed at.

"There is a loading dock and then steps to make it onto the boat. Don't worry. It's perfectly safe."

His breathing began to calm, less intense but still fast. Hyperventilating had decreased but he was still unsure.

"We'll hold your hand," Sandra tried to calm him.

"All aboard!" the captain called out.

"'Bout time!" a familiar voice shouted.

Through the throng of people, Daniel noticed a bald, slightly overweight, middle-aged man standing next to a woman, presumably his wife. Surrounding them were four kids. One of which also looked familiar.

"Shit," Daniel cursed under his breath.

"What is it, honey?" Sandra asked.

"Nothing. Just that guy over there."

"The one who shouted?" Sandra raised an eyebrow.

"Mhm," Daniel continued. "We met him at the restroom. Not a bad guy, just a lot of questions."

"Vacations are never really vacations anymore," Sandra chuckled.

"No. Vacations are just never permanent."

Soon, the passengers were boarding at a medium pace. When the Brightly family's turn came, Joseph was apprehensive but still went with them. He only stalled on the first couple of steps.

"I told you it'd be alright," Sandra smiled.

"Yeah, I guess you were right." Joseph pushed his glasses further up on his face. His next fear was losing them over the side.

McGrew and his family came shortly after. It did not take him long to find the Brightlys. Daniel thought he had to have sniffed them out because they were near the bow but far back from the pulpit.

"Hey! Doctor!" he called out to Daniel.

"Erm, Professor."

"Right. Right. I'm sorry." He looked over his shoulder. "Honey, this is the marine biologist I was telling you about."

The haggard, overweight woman moseyed on over. "Oh yes, the fish doctor."

Sandra managed to suppress a laugh. Her face could not hide it though.

"What's so funny?" McGrew's wife asked.

"Hmm?" Sandra turned to her. "Nothing. I've never heard someone call him that. I think it's funny."

"Well, that's what he is, isn't he?"

"I study fish. I don't treat their diseases," Daniel said as upbeat as he could.

"Forgive my wife," McGrew said. "She watches too much television."

Suddenly, one of his children, a little girl, bumped into him. "Daddy. Can we sit up top?"

"Sit wherever you'd like. It's a big boat." McGrew glared at Daniel as if it were a challenge.

Daniel looked away.

When they went back around the starboard side, he exhaled loudly.

Sandra giggled. "Good job."

"Thank you."

"You kept a straight face like you were playing poker." She nudged him. "I can see why you don't like him."

They were underway within ten minutes of everyone boarding. Joseph noticed the other boat was devoid of people.

"Why isn't that one coming with us?"

"It'll go when this boat comes back," Sandra explained.

Meanwhile, Daniel was in his element. The salty air smelled wonderful as the sea breeze brushed gently across his pale face. He breathed in through his nose and out through his mouth. Being cooped up at that campsite had been becoming more of a chore than a pleasure. Despite how much he enjoyed the outdoors, the sea was his preferred natural nourishment.

This was his kind of vacation.

CHAPTER FIVE

A familiar ballet.

Craig Brinston had not been diving in years let alone in the ocean. With his job as a theater teacher, he was constantly battling for time off. It was a choice between the underwater world and the real world. He could easily lose himself down in the wide-open depths of the sea. He was never one to let things get in the way of that.

That all changed when he had a child.

His daughter, from a very young age, was enthusiastic about her dad's interest and hobbies. At age two they caught her dancing to some operatic piece. The older she got, the more fluid her motions had become. She was now nine and one of his top students over at Brinston's Ballet and Dance. His wife, Kendra, was in charge of the graceful tutu skirt donning kids. He was more interested in the younglings finding and expressing themselves through art. Kendra tried to get their child to do ballet. She stuck close to her dad and his involvement.

After he donned his flippers, Craig's feet flopped into the waves. He felt like a buffoon but knew what he was doing. As the water grew deeper, he peeked below. Looking through his prescription goggles, he saw the drop off. One of the many that Martha's Vineyard was known for.

Placing the regulator in his mouth, he leaned forward and began to glide across the surface. Following this, he spread his arms out and began to push through the choppy water. This was not for recreation but, rather, for dinner.

He had heard about some lobster being spotted near the estuary from a reliable local friend and wanted to see for himself. The man had never let him down before. Craig was by no means an islander, but he was a frequent visitor.

On his side, he had a bag to stuff the crustaceans in. He was already noticing movement on the bottom. Approaching a pile of rocks, he took a deep breath of air through the tube. He took one last look at the surface. The water was not as erratic now. There were no strong currents here. Perfect for a free dive.

Descending in the same manner he swam topside with, his journey took him down no more than twelve feet. He reached out and lifted one of the lighter rocks. Nothing. He continued to investigate through the pile. Some small gaps between the stones caught his eye as well as movement within. Grabbing the bag from his hip, he silently cursed himself for not having something to get ahold of them with. Reaching inside now, he found that the pocket was warm. There was definitely something in there, either feeding or nesting. He felt the shell-shaped tail and tugged.

A monster lobster came free from its hiding place. It was large for the area. If Craig were to guess, it was nearly two feet long. It snapped wildly but was unable to arch its back enough to pinch any part of his body as he held it out. He examined it. It was rather aggressive. Usually when he grabbed hold of a lobster it was slow. The pincers were snapping wildly every which way.

He had no idea he was holding out dinner.

Something snatched it. It was so fast that his mind could not even process what had happened before the lobster was gone. His mind snapped into survival mode, and he darted for the surface. The sheer pressure building up in his head made him want to stop. Instinct for self-preservation took over. Blood began to expel from his nose and mouth as he experienced the bends.

***

Stanley never knew why he had not received the captain title. He knew everything, maybe even a little more, than Burt did. It was becoming old hat at this point. He did everything the man told him to do. Stuff that involved fishing, boat maintenance, and beyond. He fancied himself the mirror image of Burt. Lately, the very idea of that was becoming a drag.

As their boat, Lady Lace, chugged through the calm waters near the estuary, the tranquility of the environment brought about a sense of ease for the young fisherman. He did not get many of these moments. When he did, he embraced them. He closed his eyes and envisioned a nice shrimp scampi on a plate served with garlic bread. It made his stomach grumble just thinking about it. The sea and its inhabitants brought relief and nourishment to him the likes no woman or paycheck could.

"Don't worry. We'll get you ashore, ya landlubber," Burt called down to him from the helm.

Peace of mind broken, Stanley glared at Burt as the man picked up his Styrofoam cup and produced blackened spittle into it. He was repulsed by the sight. Burt noticed.

"Puts hair on your balls."

"I'm sure Pabst Blue Ribbon does too."

Burt scoffed at the very idea. "Shit's for pussies."

"What's the matter, little can with some glowing lights scare ya?"

"Boy, the only thing scaring me is the sea herself."

"You have to enjoy nature's splendors."

"Okay, ya fuckin' hippy."

Stanley laughed. "Okay, shore thing. You'll be back at home with Mrs. Grove soon. Now there's a lady I would not like to see in lace."

"Don't remind me," Burt chuckled and reached for his nearby flask of bourbon.

He then noticed something or someone out by the shoreline. There was a small speedboat situated pretty close to the sandbank. Next to it was clearly a man snorkeling. His body was face down and he was not moving. A bit of an odd sight.

"Look at that fool. He could've just as easily walked into the ocean to scuba dive if he was planning on going out only that far," Burt laughed cynically.

Stanley looked over and saw the man. Something worried him though. His air regulator was being flooded with water with each passing wavelet. "I think he's unconscious."

Burt made his way over to the portside and leaned over to examine the scene more. "Aye, maybe you're right."

"What do we do?"

"What do you mean what do we do? You should know the procedures."

"Call the coastguard, yeah," Stanley explained. "By the time they get here though, he'll be dead for sure."

The captain thought on it briefly. "Alright. I'll call it in. You reach for him with the net."

Stanley was about to complain that he never got to do the cool things but found the timing would be inappropriate. He made his way over to the gunwale and unclipped the six-foot-long net from the portside. He could hear Burt barking orders as if he had any authority in the situation. Stanley looked down at the net and remembered the man did have some say and it involved him.

He silently wished it were the other way around.

With a firm grip, he extended the net over the side. The first time landed with a small splash about a foot and a half away from the fellow. The second was a bit closer but off too far to the left.

"Ah, sonofabitch," he cursed quietly.

There was rippling in the water near the body. Small waves brushed against it. Stanley deduced they were from the boat coming up next to the corpse and his frequent splashing. The third time, he managed to snag him around the air regulator. *Of course.*

It only took a single light pull and it became dislodged from the man's mouth.

"What's taking you so long, Reed?" Burt called down to him again.

"You need to get closer."

"No can do. I don't want to get stuck on the embankment," Burt continued. "Coastguard said they'd be out here in quarter of an hour. We should just sit tight."

"I can't just leave the guy," Stanley said.

He heard weighted boots come down on the deck with a resounding thud. Burt appeared next to Stanley.

"Give me that." The captain tore the net away from the first mate.

As he dragged it in, he began to chuckle. "Guess he didn't need it."

"I'll just hop in and get him." Stanley swung a leg over the side.

"If you're dinner, I ain't payin'," Burt said matter-of-factly.

Stanley repositioned himself back on the deck. "What's that supposed to mean?"

The wheels in his head were clearly turning and Burt was loving every minute of it. He then jabbed a finger in the dead man's direction. "You think something killed him?"

"Maybe. Or maybe he got spooked by something, had a heart attack or experienced the bends."

"I'm voting for the latter. I don't see any bite marks."

Burt grinned cheekily. "I guess we'll find out when the coastguard gets here. How much you want to bet he was almost chow?"

"You can pay for my dinner when it's revealed he drowned."

"Fair enough."

The two shook on it.

It was ten minutes later when the coastguard's vessel approached. Both men aboard the Lady Lace were doing chores of different varying difficulties. Burt was busy looking over his log of daily catches. Today would be a bad day for any potential catch. He could already feel it in his bones. He had begun watching Stanley swab the deck when he saw the other boat approach. There were a few crew members aboard. Each one looked uninterested yet alert. It was clear they were dedicated to their jobs, but they had seen this before. At least, that's what they presumably figured.

The coastguard's boat pulled up to the portside of the smaller, emptier speedy. They looked it over as if to see if anything of value was aboard.

Burt cupped his hands over his mouth. "We get to salvage her, right?"

They paid no mind.

"So much for first come first serve," Stanley stated.

"Where's the body?" one of the crew called back.

"It's…" Stanley pointed to the spot where he last saw it. "I don't know. I think it drifted away."

"Shit," they heard one of them mumble.

"We'll have to scope out the area," the first guy shouted again. "Can you two stick around?"

"I don't know. We've got a pretty busy day, and…"

"…Yes, we can," Stanley cut him off mid-sentence.

"The island owes you one."

"Why not the government?" Burt called back, only half-joking.

No response.

Making their way around the ship, two of the crew were getting some gear together while the third kept his eyes glued to the water. Every wave looked like it carried a dark secret. Black masses rolled in conjunction with the water movement. Every ripple held a secret. Yet none of them would fall for it. The false alarms were easy to catch when staring at the sea for so long.

Burt was growing bored by the time both men donned their scuba suits and equipment.

"See anything?" one of them could be heard asking.

"Nope," the other on the upper deck stated.

"Alright. We'll have a quarter-hour look."

Swinging their legs over the edge, they were both about to hop over when something came up at them. It was a horrifying sight. The jaws agape, eyes staring into their souls.

"Fuck!" one of the frogmen shouted.

"Oh shit," the man at the helm said flatly.

"Found him," the third guy said.

Burt was somewhat enthusiastic. "So, can we go now?"

"We need statements at the very least," one of them said. Burt could not tell who.

"Goddamnit," he spat.

"How'd he die?" Stanley asked before thinking not to.

"Looks like," one of the frog men leaned over and examined the body, "he's got blood coming out of his nose and mouth. I'd say he experienced the bends."

Stanley smirked and looked up at Burt. "Looks like ya owe me a free meal."

***

As Vernon Hackery finished up his morning thermos of coffee, he was already feeling anxious. Not for what he was about to see or experience. Rather the idea of being out of caffeine for the time being. It was making his head hurt. He had filled it not long before heading out for the day. Now the giant cup was down to the last few sips.

There was a time he did not drink coffee. In fact, he only drank water and juice. When his wife was still alive, everything seemed simpler. With her gone, it all came apart. He lived for caffeine and nicotine. Speaking of which, he wanted to light up. Part of him told him to wait until he got to Grant's farm. The other little devil on his right shoulder told him to just take a few hits. He was not arresting anyone. No one would smell it.

He managed to fight the urge when the gate to the property came into view. Whispering a silent prayer, he was about to honk his horn when his CB radio went off.

"Sheriff, this is headquarters. We have a 10-32. I repeat we have a 10-32. Over."

Vernon reached for the radio and clicked the button on the receiver. "What's the status on them? Over."

"Deceased. The coastguard is requesting a police presence. Too many onlookers. Over."

"My ETA is about half an hour. Is there anyone else closer who can cover? Over."

"Negative. Everyone else is out on active duty. Over."

"Understood. Sheriff out."

"Copy that. Over and out."

Placing the receiver back on the cradle, he looked ahead at the gate. There was no one there. He cursed to himself before shifting to reverse. Before he could change his mind, he was already more than halfway down the path and making his way back onto the main road.

“Damned island’s always full of surprises,” Vernon said to himself.

CHAPTER SIX

The tour of a lifetime.

Seeing such a youthful presence enjoying the island always brought happiness to Morgan. There were not many youngsters who found such interest in the film as he did himself when he was a kid. The magic of cinema had long been forgotten over the decades. Such a phenomenon only occurred once and Jaws was lightning in a bottle as far as he was concerned.

Devon's grandfather seemed interested too. Perhaps not as much. As the tour went on, he found solace in the colorful location. It all felt so alive with the throng of people walking the streets and the gift shops that were around every corner. Morgan had asked if he had ever been to Martha's Vineyard. The short answer, no. The long answer, he had never been on a tour of a film location. It was surprisingly not Devon's first time. He had visited Universal Studios last summer with his parents.

"So tell me how much you know about the making of Jaws, Devon?" Morgan asked.

"No more than the average fan," he chuckled.

"Well then you're in for a true treat!" replying cheerfully, Morgan looked into the rearview mirror briefly. Both tourists' eyes were glued to the windows. They marveled at the location for all its natural and manmade splendor.

"Would you like to see the town hall?"

"Can I go in?" Devon inquired.

"Yes. It's free to the public."

"Oh, heck yeah!" the boy cheered.

Morgan brought the van towards Main Street. He then passed a few homes. He quickly pointed to one ahead.

"Do you see that house?"

"Yes," both of them replied in unison.

"That's where the police station and Gazette was located in the film. Further down we'll see the town hall."

It was not long before they drove towards the government building. Morgan turned down a nearby street where a parking lot was located. "Anyone want something to drink? Coffee, water?"

"I could use some caffeine," Buckley smiled.

"There's a coffee shop down here. We can walk over to the town hall from there."

"Sounds great!" Devon smiled.

Espresso Love was already busy. Both tourists and selectmen and women alike were in line. Devon's smile beamed at the sight of everyone. He wanted to thank everyone for not changing the island too much but fought the urge. It was becoming difficult to contain himself now.

"What would you like?" Buckley asked his grandson.

"Can I get some water?"

"Of course."

After they got their beverages, Buckley went over to add flavor to his coffee. He had acquired a distinct love of caramel thanks to his daughter. He reached for the dark, syrupy liquid and squeezed some from the bottle into his drink. As he did so, he noticed the word *Honey* labeled on it. At first, he was annoyed but then shrugged and was surprised to find it did not taste half bad. After adding two sugars to it, he turned to Devon and, together, they followed Morgan back out.

Devon stood beside his grandfather as they made their way over to the big white building. He did not even realize that Morgan was not with them. He had stayed by the van to let them experience it themselves.

Walking through the front door, it seemed a bit unfamiliar until they narrowed their sights on the hallway. As they walked down it, it was as if the movie were playing out before them. Soon, they were in the meeting room. The sun lit the room making it feel warm and wholesome. Devon felt a sense of belonging. Buckley looked up.

"I never realized there was a window up there."

Both stared at the ceiling. It gave the room a glow that only Mother Earth could provide. Devon then looked down and was able to pinpoint where everything was. The room was changed around over the years, but the esthetic was the same.

"You ready?"

"No," Devon answered. He was absorbed.

"Let me know when."

Buckley backed up and raised his camera. He took a picture of Devon in the room and grinned. The generations the film had an impact on would be felt for more to come.

As they exited the town hall, Morgan was just finishing his beverage. They approached him and got in the van.
"Looks pretty similar, huh?"

"Feels it," Devon said softly.

Pulling out of the parking lot, Morgan smiled. "How about some of the beach locations?"

Devon was already amazed by the simplicity of the government building. Buckley thought he might lose his mind when he got to see some of the areas where the shark was truly involved.

"Let's go!" the young boy cheered.

"Alrighty! We'll probably be going out of order, but we'll head to the bridge and then the locations where Treysie was eaten."

"Perfect! Maybe we'll see some blonde babes there too," Buckley howled with laughter.

"This time of year, ya never know. We'll probably see some kids jumping off the bridge though. That much I can almost guarantee."

Immediately, Buckley felt his grandson's eyes on him. He slowly turned his head.

"Grandpa. Can I?"

"Your mother would have my head."

"She would have your head if I drove a car or stole something. I just want to jump into some water."

"I don't think it's a good idea."

"It's not that high above the water," Devon pleaded his case. "I've been on rollercoasters that were more dangerous. That was only last year!"

Buckley looked to Morgan to see if he would back him up. Instead, the man just pointed. "Over there is where Quint bought his piano wire."

Devon looked but did not seem as enthusiastic. He felt as though it was a right of passage to jump in that water to honor the film.

"When we get there, if I deem it safe, then maybe." Buckley could not even finish his sentence when the boy launched himself into his arms.

"Thank you, Grandpa!"

"Maybe!" he repeated.

"It'll be safe! I'm a strong swimmer."

"That's not what worries me. It's the distance you'll hit the water from."

"Just don't dive," Morgan explained. "I don't remember how deep the water is."

"Thanks," Buckley told the man.

"Just telling you the truth."

"This is going to be fun!" Devon cheered loudly.

"I hope I don't regret this."

So do I, Morgan thought as he drove them down towards the pond area.

Pulling up to the side of the road, Morgan put the van in park. Devon wanted to hop out and run around, his adrenaline making him giddy with excitement. Buckley put a hand on the boy's shoulder. He told him to relax as he himself did deep breathing exercises.

"I hope we see a shark!" Devon exclaimed.

"It's not entirely impossible." Morgan smiled, trying to sound confident that they would but not so much so that it was more than a possibility.

He got out and made his way around the vehicle. Popping open the doors, Devon practically fell out, catching himself mid tumble.

"Are you alright?" Morgan reached out to help him.

"I'm alright."

"Okay." He made sure the boy was able to get down.

Buckley got out and inhaled the warm salty air. It was a different kind of odor than he was used to.

"Smells like cow manure."

"That's just the sea," Morgan chuckled. "It can take some getting used to."

The three then made their way across the road when the coast was clear. Devon could see a bunch of kids jumping off the bridge. They plummeted in like a needle through water. His eyes grew wide.

"There are no sharks! The kids are in the water and are fine."

Buckley glanced at the bridge. "Too high."

"But Grandpa! You said!"

"I didn't guarantee. That is way too high up for you to jump. Those kids have to be eleven or twelve."

Devon looked over at them. "They look about the same age as me."

His grandfather shook his head. "I don't think it's a good idea. Maybe in a couple of years when you're older."

"It's the fiftieth anniversary!" Devon whined.

Looking from the bridge to Devon, he felt torn. Then he looked at Morgan. "Is it safe?"

"Kids do it all day long. Younger than him even." Morgan wanted to be truthful. He was beginning to feel as if he were getting between something that he should not have to be involved in.

Buckley looked at Morgan with disdain. His face told him he would not receive a good tip. The old man then rolled his eyes.

"You better not hit your head."

Devon's whole face lit up. "Make sure to get me on camera!"

"I was hoping I wouldn't have to," he replied.

Before anyone could oppose, Devon was running alongside the bridge sidewalk. He tore his shirt off and kicked off his slides. The other kids seemed to not mind his presence. They even let him cut in line.

Helplessly watching, Buckley saw his grandson climb over the side and look down. He did not seem afraid but, rather, in awe of the water below. He held his nose and took a deep breath. Buckley raised his camera and waited for the perfect shot. Devon leapt forward, jumping out towards the water. His legs did not swing or flop. He just dove feet first, straight down. The splash was nothing spectacular. His grandfather immediately searched the water for the boy to resurface.

"How deep is it?" Buckley asked, kicking himself for not getting clarification.

"No deeper than a pool," Morgan replied.

A few seconds passed; momentary stillness came over Buckley. He wondered how long Devon could hold his breath for. For that matter, he was not sure the boy could even swim. His parents' kiddy pool did not count. Fifteen seconds had passed now. A whole quarter of a minute. He was past worried. He was beginning to panic.

"Do you see him?" Morgan called suddenly to the boys on the bridge.

This made Buckley's demeanor change. It only got worse when they shook their heads.

"I'm going in," Buckley told the tour guide.

"I'll go with you," Morgan stated.

The two men began to make their way alongside the rocks and towards the road.

Devon surfaced then. He was not alone.

"Grandpa! Look what I found!" He held aloft the severed tail of what was a huge lobster.

"Treyt almighty, boy! You scared the hell out of me!" Buckley exclaimed.

"Sorry, Grandpa. It's like a whole different world down there!"

"Come ashore. Let's get you dried off."

"Aw, do I have to?"

"Yes. Please."

Devon began for the shore. He was halfway there when he noticed there was no real easy way to get up on the rocks.

"I'll go past the bridge for an easier spot to get ashore," he explained.

"It's not much easier on that side," Morgan told him.

Buckley made his way onto the rocks and scouted the area. There was a beach nearby. "Go towards there. We'll meet you over…"

He paused.

"Where?" Devon was whipping water off his face after a small wave brushed against him.

"What in the hell is that?" Buckley shouted.

A dark mass glided just below the surface. It was huge, the size of a school bus but leaner. It seemed to be perusing the area.

"It's probably a whale or something," Morgan stated.

"A whale!" one of the kids on the bridge shouted with glee. "I've always wanted to swim with a whale."

Two followed him as they jumped off a bridge.

Buckley returned his attention to Devon. "I don't think it's a whale."

Devon wanted to argue but saw the horrified expression on his grandfather's face and began towards him.

That's when the screaming started.

By the time Buckley got Devon up out of the water, two of the boys had already disappeared below the surface. The sea churned with a frothing red coating the surface.

"Get out of the water!" Morgan screamed.

The third child was the one who wanted to swim with the assumed whale in the first place. He began to make a beeline for where Devon got out. Buckley was already off the rocks, cradling his grandson.Morgan charged up the rocks, hoping between the gaps with ease. He held his hand out for the boy to grab hold.

"C'mon! Hurry up!" he pleaded for him.

A nauseating feeling washed over Morgan as he saw the water settle from where the others were taken. Now the dark shape was chasing down this one.

"Give me your hand!"

The child was so close. Just a few more strokes and he would be within grabbing distance. Morgan extended his arm out as far as he could. He strained himself but was in protection mode. This child was in harm's way. It was instinctive to try and help him. The boy was now reaching out. Morgan managed to get a loose grip on his hand. It slipped just as some creature bit down around his legs. All Morgan could see were the teeth and what appeared to be the mouth of some large blue crocodile. It tore the boy away from him and dragged him out to sea. A crimson trail followed.

CHAPTER SEVEN

A perfect home.

It had hibernated in a small section of pond for many years. A crevasse at the bottom was all that it required, having burrowed its way inside. During the colder seasons, its nostrils miraculously did not freeze. The heat its body radiated was enough to warm the little nook it dwelled in. A natural incubator for its tired body. The perfect home for the perfect predator.

Now that it was awake, it had to feed. The lobster was but the smallest of morsels. A scrap in the plethora of prey that surrounded its new scouting areas. All along the channel, it had scooped up such tiny treats. After consuming three larger targets, it was now satiated enough to return to its original habitat to rest again.

This time would not be so long.

Boom.

Another explosion nearby. The third one that day.

***

"As we build new housing, it's always important to not take too much of the environment down in the process," Bill Owen announced to the group of people behind him.

They all seemed intrigued by the processes that the mayor had implemented to keep the integrity of the area intact.

Controlled explosions were detonated in only key locations where pipes could be implemented to have working septic systems and running water from manmade wells. It was a process, but Owen assured them it would be a rewarding one. The neighbors mostly did not mind as long as they kept off their property.

Two that did have an issue with the process were Kane Grant and Keith Sturges. They were situated right next to Farm Pond. It was prime real estate. The likes of which Bill hoped to purchase one day. In the meantime, he would just have to put up with their antics.

The mayor turned to the group, investors from the mainland. Some wanted to work in the food industry while others were more interested in buying up one of the properties. They would no doubt exchange cards and information long before the tour was over. All eyes were on Bill now.

"We are nearing Farm Pond. This is mainly called Grant's place by the locals but a fellow farmer, Sturges, co-owns the property with him. There is, unfortunately, not much space to build here as it is mostly their property," he continued. "Where we are standing is the starting point. About a mile of land is not theirs and can be bought and used. It's a pleasant area, quaint and tranquil."

Boom.

"Well, for the most part," Bill chuckled. "Construction will hopefully cease by the end of the year. That'll give you enough time in between to settle in and get things ready for the next planter season."

"What's that?" a woman amongst the group pointed over down some ways.

Bill looked over in the direction she was gesturing to. "Why, that's Farm Pond, my dear."

"I know that. I mean, what's that in the water?"

"I don't see anything, Darla," a man, presumably her husband, claimed.

"That's probably ol' Vannessa poking her head out to say hello," a voice came from behind Bill.

He spun around to see Kane Grant standing there with a look on his face that told him he was not welcome.

"What are you doing?" Bill said, bitterly.

"I live here."

"Well, if you don't mind, I'm in the middle of a presentation."

"Who's Vannessa?" Darla asked.

"A legend 'round here. A serpent of the pond. She comes out every so often. Me and my buddy, Keith, saw her the other day. Speaking of which, Mayor. I need to talk to you 'bout somthin'."

"Later."

"How about now?" Kane continued. "Why didn't the sheriff come out here when we called this morning? Could have been something serious."

"My apologies. There were other matters to attend to."

"I'm sure. Crowd control. Booze hounds. Makes sense," Kane chuckled.

"If you don't mind, I'd like to continue the tour," Bill told the farmer.

"Alright. Just don't say I didn't try." Kane backed away and then made his way back down the hill towards his home.

"What a strange fellow," Darla stated.

"They're harmless. Just like Farm Pond. This area is totally and completely safe."

Kane could feel their eyes on him as he marched inside his house. It was not something to poke around in, that pond. To him, it was justifiable to have warned them, even if in a passive way. *What they know now may make them reconsider.*

He slowly made his way over towards one of the windows in the small homestead and saw the group laughing with Bill. His blood pressure began to rise. It had not done so in a long time. The very thought that his warning was tossed aside like an old newspaper made his deep-rooted hatred for modern humanity bloom even more.

"I ain't no laughing stock!" Kane exclaimed as he marched over towards the dining area.

His home was simple to say the least. A fireplace took center stage inside with his rooms surrounding it. The kitchen was on the left when walking in and he had a hammock set up near a window on the right. In front of that was a stack of wood for the fireplace, neatly stacked and ready for the flames. To his left near the door was the dining room. It was nothing fancy. It had two chairs. The other was a spare. He would occasionally have Keith over if he had a good set of steaks and had harvested some nice corn. Other than that, it was practically an empty household.

Taking a seat in the chair, he took a few deep breaths. In through his nose and out his mouth. He once thought he was not a temperamental man. Having contact with outsiders usually had this effect on him. Besides Keith, he did not care for anyone. He barely fancied Keith as it was. The man spent more time in the bottle than his field. Their land was a stark contrast.

Bill had come by during the last harvest season to tell Keith to maintain his property better. For once, Kane had taken his side. Had he known it was to impress potential investors and landowners, he would have handled it differently. He was not sure why Bill was even handling this gig. He figured one of the young whippersnappers from college would jump at the opportunity to push the sale. Knowing Bill, there was an ulterior motive behind why he was here.

Managing to calm himself down, he stood up. He went back over towards the window and saw that they were all gone. He then looked back down at

Farm Pond. The placid water had an eeriness to it he had not experienced in years. Perhaps Vanessa was back. Or perhaps, he was just getting too old and growing increasingly mad.

***

The ferry docked in the harbor. It looked similar to the one in Nantucket. McGrew and his family were some of the first to get off. The large man inhaled, welcoming the scent of the island community.

"Happy fiftieth!" he shouted.

Some of the passengers cheered in response. Others who did not were most likely too nervous or here for a different reason. Either way, Daniel and his family made their way towards the steps. This time, Joseph was less timid than before. He made it offboard with ease. Daniel figured his son was just ecstatic to be there. In a place he had only seen in the film.

Sandra was quick to get off. She had begun to grow nauseous during the trip, using the bathroom several times during the short journey out. Daniel knew she barely had her sea legs and could get motion sickness from time to time. It was a curse as far as she was concerned. It had really gotten bad when she had Covid a few years prior. The shock to her system was instant and she had yet to fully recover.

With most of the passengers off the boat, they made their way towards the main transport area. There were several shops and restaurants as well as a large map to help guide people as to where to go and how to get there.

It was growing increasingly warm out. Borderline hot. They made it a few hundred yards before they found an information center. There was an ice cream stop that Jospeh began to eye intently. Sandra took a seat on one of the benches while Daniel looked over the map. The whole time, Joseph eyed the ice cream stand.

"We'll get some in a moment," Daniel told him without looking. He could tell the boy wanted a chocolate sundae. They were his favorite, and it was written on the chalkboard above the cashier's head.

"Okay," he replied, disappointed.

"We're at Vineyard Haven now. It should take us less than ten minutes to get to the hospital from here," Daniel explained as his finger trailed over the map.

"Good, maybe they'll have some Dramamine." Sandra stood up and made her way over to them.

"I'm sure they can spare some," Daniel told her.

"Can we get some ice cream now?" Joseph asked.

Daniel smiled at him. "I'll call us a cab. Then we can get some."

Joseph nodded. "Alright."

***

The day had only gotten worse for Bill Owen. He had tried desperately to get some negotiations underway but only managed one couple. Darla and Colt Ferling. They were not too old and could easily handle farm life. Presumably better than Keith or Kane.

Damn that Kane, always trying to ruin everything.

Ever since he found out that Kane was not on his side when it came to industrialization and homes being brought in, there had been tension between the two. Now he had gotten in the way of several potential buyers. He figured he would have to visit the islanders when he got back to whomever had been blowing up his cell phone.

Looking at the caller ID, he was even more stressed. He had dreaded the day he gave Deputy Rosenthal his own personal number. With Sheriff Hackery's declining mental state, it seemed for the best at the time. He quickly dialed the man's number and waited for the ring.

It did not even get a chance as a man answered with bated breath. "Mayor. We've got a situation here. Over."

"This isn't a radio so stall the technical jargon and tell me why the hell you're calling me?"

"The sheriff informed me to do so. There are too many screaming parents he's trying to calm down. I guess he didn't want me to say the wrong thing."

"Screaming parents? What's happening? Where are you?"

Rosenthal took a deep breath. "We're at the Sengekontacket Circle. Over by the bridge. Mayor, some kids were just killed by what's being reported as a giant shark, crocodile, or something."

CHAPTER EIGHT

Out of the loop.

If anyone told Anthony Butler that seeing an old friend after so long would be a lukewarm experience, he would have called their bluff. Walking through the malfunctioning doors though, Daniel Brightly and his family entered the hospital. The commotion took them by surprise. Several people were in the lobby with looks that could be described as ashen with disbelief covering their pale faces. Some mumbled while others were silent.

Most of the nurses were talking with them though not getting much response. The stricken families were at a loss. A couple of toddlers played in the toy center, unaware of the gravity of the situation their parents and other family members now faced. One of the paramedics had come in from the front office. He was just signing out for shift change when Anthony stopped him. They exchanged words. The ambulance driver seemed annoyed but nodded regardless.

Daniel had taken in enough of the mournful scene before him and made his way over towards the doctor. Anthony regarded him cooly. He did not speak right away, uncertain if he should do so. Instead, he decided to usher Daniel down the hallway, past the service desk. His graven look was almost more than the marine biologist could bear.

"What happened?" Daniel asked finally.

"Apparently, three children were killed by a shark."

"What!" Dan's voice rose a few octaves too high.

Anthony gestured for him to lower his voice by lowering his hands.

"When did this happen?" Daniel asked, quieter now.

"About half an hour ago. They were jumping off the bridge. Eyewitness reports say that they thought a whale was in the water and they wanted to swim with it."

"A whale? How big, did anyone get a look at it?" Daniel inquired.

"One man saw a shadow. The other saw something else."

"What did he see?" Daniel asked.

"Teeth, Daniel. Very big teeth."

A sudden scream echoed down the hallway. Both men snapped in the direction of the hysterical woman. She cried out for her child. The shock of it all was taking effect. Anthony and Daniel quickly made their way out into the lobby. Sandra was holding Joseph close. Both were petrified of the woman, knees on the ground, hands clasped in prayer. A nearby man, her husband, quickly helped her to her feet.

"He can't be gone!" she sobbed deeply.

"I'm sorry." He cradled his wife and repeated, "I'm so sorry."

"Why weren't you there?"

"I was on the beach down the other end."

"You were fishing!" She spat literal saliva in his face as she pushed away.

"I was watching him the whole time," the man shouted back. "No one saw it. It just happened!"

Burying her hands in her face, the woman began to dry heave.

"Can we get a bucket over here! Please!" the man begged one of the nurses.

Anthony turned to Daniel and then looked beyond him at his family. "I'm going to give her a sedative. I want you to bring your family to my home. Do you remember where it is?"

"Yes," Daniel said with a sullen expression.

The woman screamed wildly. Joseph dropped his ice cream.

"My baby!" She went into hysterics. "You let my baby die!"

She began to beat her husband on the chest and arms. The toddlers began to cry as the adults began to feel her stress and express it slowly.

Daniel scooped up Joseph and Sandra quickly followed. When they got to the sliding doors, they wouldn't open. Daniel stomped his foot down in front of them, but they failed to operate.

"Doc! I need some help here!"

"Damn doors!" Anthony was seething. He had predicted something would happen that would cause distress with those doors.

The paramedic, tall and lean, hurried over and preformed an override. They slid open and the three hurried through.

"What else can go wrong?" Anthony said and then immediately kicked himself for saying it. Things could always get worse. He knew this, as did everyone else in the hospital, on this island.

***

As Bill Owen drove down the road to the estuary, the previous conversation with the deputy stuck in his head. *A shark, a crocodile, or something.* Whatever had killed those kids was probably long gone but he was going to take every precaution to keep the beaches and water safe.

Damage control was considered. In fact, it was what he was thinking about most. The loss of three children would not only deeply affect the islanders and tourists but it would not look good on the community as a whole. Especially not when the anniversary of that movie was just around the corner. It could not have been worse timing.

The deputy waved him down and then guided his car towards a parking area.

"I know where I'm going, dipshit!" he told him, scathingly.

"Sorry," Rosenthal said ashamedly.

Bill was not about to let up on him. "Where did this happen exactly? Where's the sheriff? Why are you directing traffic instead of taking statements?"

It was as if Rosenthal had become overwhelmed with the barrage of questions. A few precious seconds passed as he tried to find answers for every inquiry he had been asked.

"Right below the bridge. The sheriff is, uh," He turned and looked, "I think he's on the other side of the bridge. Oh, and there's no one else to get statements from."

"If the sheriff's over there, why did you have me park here?"

"I… Uh."

"For Treysake!" He rolled up his window and drove back and then across the bridge.

Sure enough, Vernon Hackery was looking over the area on the other side. Bill got out and slammed the door. The action did not startle the sheriff as much as it seemingly annoyed him. The mayor trudged through sand in his grey dress pants.

"Where are the parents?"

"I had them go to the hospital. They were all a wreck, understandably. I had the most stable ones drive."

"Then why do you need me here? I should be with them. You know, consoling the community."

"There is something you need to see," Vernon told him.

"Oh. What's that?" Bill asked, barely enthusiastic.

Vernon made his way over to a set of rocks. He pulled out the bottom of a lobster tail.

"Having that for dinner?"

The sheriff then dug inside the tail. Squishing, meshy sounds could be heard as his whole fist practically fit inside.

"What the hell are you doing?"

He did not answer. Instead, he pulled back. In his grasp was an object he retrieved. He walked over and placed it on a rock where another one was. Bill took a step closer.

"Are those rocks? Spearheads? What?"

"Teeth."

Bill's face turned red. "Teeth?"

"I'm not an expert, but those don't look like rocks to me."

"What kind of animal around here would have teeth like that?"

"Crocodile, probably."

"A crocodile? Don't they live in swamps?"

"Saltwater crocodile."

"This is ridiculous!" Bill shouted. "First your idiot deputy has been driving all over hell and creation to find you and, when *I* do, you have stories of crocodiles."

"I can't guarantee that it's a crocodile. Like I said, I'm not an expert. I can say though that if this community thinks it's a shark, it's a shark."

"What?" Bill looked at him with confusion.

"I'm saying that it'll be open season on sharks. That means every drunkard with a boat will be out there trying to catch the potential man, erm, child eater."

"This is ridiculous!"

"No, what would be ridiculous is if you ignore these." Vernon grabbed the teeth and held them out to the mayor.

Bill looked at him with a cold stare. "Crocodile or shark. The beaches will have to be closed."

"That doesn't stop an all-out hunt."

"Maybe we'll put up a bounty on the fish."

"Bad idea."

"How's that?" Bill smirked.

"You've seen the movie. You know how that'd go."

"That was a work of fiction. I think everything was possible until they went out to hunt the shark. Then it got a bit ridiculous."

"If you say so." Vernon shook his head.

"I know so. My dad used to fish in this area long before that monster hit movie. He never saw anything like that happen around here."

"Regardless. I would just wait for it to go away. Cut off its food supply entirely."

"Not happening. This ends sooner rather than later."

Bill turned on his heels and stormed back up to the bridge.

"What happens if it doesn't? We'll be out of this island's busiest season yet."

"Don't worry. I have an idea for that too."

CHAPTER NINE

It was unfathomable.

As Burt Groves squeezed the ketchup bottle, allowing the shiny red substance to lather his plate, his eyes seemed to take on a frenzied look. One that Stanley often attributed to as a serious case of the crimson chip craving. He wanted to gag or turn away. The smell of the dense salty tomato liquid brought about a reflex he was unsure he could control. The stuff on his chicken was gross enough. With his chips though. That was a whole different kind of vile.

Once the ritual was complete, he smiled devilishly at his plate. His grin reminded Stanley of the Cheshire Cat from *Alice in Wonderland*; insidious yet methodical. Burt then searched his plate for the perfect chip to start with. Stanley could only imagine if the chips had a conscience what their fearful eyes would be witnessing from below. Perhaps the flaring nostrils hovering over them like a dog on something's trail. Finally, as if to end the torture, he snagged one of the larger chips and scoffed it down.

Stanley continued to fight the urge to gag. He knew if he did, his fishing partner would call him out of it. The ketchup on chips was one thing to stomach. He did not like being called out for such his own personal distaste for something. Still, the wretched smell made his eyes water. Burt looked up and noticed before Stanley could hold back the tears.

"This shit'll put hair on your crotch."

"I hear the ladies don't like that these days."

"The ladies. Humph. Who cares what they think? Nothing but nagging trouble." Burt picked up another chip and scoffed it down.

Stanley nodded but clearly was not taking what he was saying seriously. Instead, he turned his attention to the waitress as she made her way around the tables. She was a local but had the look of a beach babe from California. Her sandy blonde hair and beaming smile had his interest. His longing to know her better kept it there.

Burt did not look up from his plate but took note of what the other was doing. "You've been staring at her for months now."

That got Stanley's attention.

"What do you know about it?"

"Well," Burt smacked his lips. "I do know I've been paying to eat here more than somewhere that serves food and beer cheap. Paying more waiting to see if you would ever grow the nerve to ask her out."

"I don't know what to say." Stanley looked down at himself.

"Clearly." His captain picked up another chip and stuffed it into his mouth.

They sat in silence for a brief time while the waitress began to head back to the kitchen. She placed an order on the ticket rack and then returned to make sure everyone's drinks were filled. Her pleasant smile warmed Stanley's heart. She soon approached their table.

"Can I get you men a refill?"

"I'm good." Burt looked at Stanley. "How 'bout you, boy?"

"I. Um. I'd like. Erm."

The waitress waited there with a patient look. Her eyes seemed to urge him to want to ask for her number, as if she was saying *Come on. Out with it. I know you want to.* Stanley looked at his water and noticed something was missing.

"Can I just get a lemon for my water?"

The waitress looked disappointed. "I'll be right back with one for ya."

He watched her go as he sulked further into his seat.

"Here. Try a chip." Burt shoved one in his face.

"Get that shit out of here," Stanley snapped at him.

Burt chuckled and chomped down on it.

A familiar face entered the joint. He was a balding fellow with a scowl that would upset children. Burt placed him among the throng of locals that were regulars at this particular dive bar. The man was someone who normally did not associate himself with these kinds of places. In fact, he had tried to condemn this place multiple times to build a condo over it. The owner had a previous record of pest infestation. It had been cleared and he had been able to keep the establishment. Burt wondered if the owner saw Bill Owen walking over to their table and, if so, would he stop him?

"Mayor! What do I owe this pleasure?"

"Cut the shit, Groves. This isn't a social call."

Stanley's attention was focused on him now. The waitress had walked towards a part of the restaurant that obstructed his view of her. He did not like that, nor did he enjoy talking with the mayor. There was no distain for the man, he just found his personality weaselly. There was always something off about him.

"Well then," Burt began. "I'll cut to the chase. I don't want what you're selling. If you think any offer you can provide will be good enough, then I suggest you double it and then double it again."

"Oh, Groves." Bill shook his head. "I think you mistook my arrival as me needing your assistance. I came here to ask a few questions. Nothing more."

"That's still needing our assistance," Stanley chuckled.

"Shut it, boy." Burt sat straight up and stared at the mayor.

"If you're here about my fishing methods, I suggest you find Ol' Wilton and disrupt his lunch."

"Wilton's not the problem. Nor is your fishing. Let's take a walk," Bill stated.

Burt looked at his food. "I'm eating."

Bill looked over the plate of chips and ketchup. "I'm sure it'll be the same as when you get back."

"Just ask me here. Whatever you have to tell me, I'm sure Stanley here can handle it."

"I need to show you something."

"I've already seen the ocean outside. I make a living off it, remember?"

"If you want to call what you do a living, I feel sorry for you," Bill said and then turned to walk away.

The captain's hand shot out and grabbed the mayor's wrist in a tight grip. "What do you know about it? Have you ever even been on a boat?"

"My dad was a fisherman. One of the best around. *Remember?*" Bill said, mockingly.

"Listen here, you little shit. I make my pay by fighting fish bigger than you."

"That's all fine and well. Right now, though, there's something that'll be destroying your catch."

"What's that?" Burt sneered.

"Let's just say, you should really take a walk with me."

The three men exited the diner. The wind was picking up a bit and a nearby fountain's water was whipping to the left and then right. The establishment was atop a high hill where the current blew strong. Bill looked over the area as they crossed the parking lot.

"Maybe it's time for Creed to relocate, huh?"

"Let's just cut to the chase," Burt snarled.

Approaching one of the nicer cars, Bill fished out his keys from his grey dress pants. He clicked the button and the doors to a black Chrysler unlocked. He opened the driver's side door. He reached into one of the cup holders and pulled out a yellowish white object. Burt and Stanley looked at it as he held it out in front of them.

"Can either of you tell me what this is?"

"Lord almighty. It looks like a tooth," Burt said instantly.

"Yeah, from a dinosaur." Stanley was baffled as well.

"No, you idiot!" Burt shouted. "If I were to guess, I'd say the damn thing belongs to a crocodile. Something big. Maybe over twenty feet."

The wind began to calm down and the sun beat down on them. Burt felt sweat pouring down his face. He was equally hot and nervous. "Where did you find this?"

"Over by the bridge at Sengekontacket Circle where three boys were killed."

Burt's face turned pale. "That's where that fellow drowned."

"Who drowned?"

"Some guy. I didn't recognize him. Coastguard came and handled it."

"Are you sure he drowned?"

"They said he experienced the bends," Stanley stated and then turned to Burt. "You still owe me a meal."

"Shut it, boy." Burt reached out and grabbed the tooth. "If this thing really belongs to a crocodile, good luck getting it to go away."

"What do you mean?" Bill asked.

"During a fishing tournament in Africa, I learned that crocodiles are very territorial. Once they get comfortable somewhere, it becomes their domain."

"You think the estuary is home to one of these creatures?"

Burt looked at the tooth as if he were staring at a picture of an old friend. "I think so."

"Then people should be safe if we close only that location," Bill suggested.

"We could probably kill it," Stanley suggested.

"I'm wondering if you have shit for brains." Burt glared at him momentarily. "You don't hunt crocodiles. They hunt you."

"What do you suggest I do?" Bill wondered with genuine concern.

"I know a guy." Burt took a deep breath. "I met him in Africa. He might be able to help."

"We don't have time to wait for someone to come here all the way from the land down under! Crocodile Dundee or no, I need this situation handled fast!"

"Then you're in luck," Burt chuckled. "Desmond is a huge fan of Jaws and is visiting for its fiftieth."

"Great!" Bill exclaimed. "Where can I find him?"

"It'd be better if you didn't. The guy's a bit out there."

"I think I can handle him." Bill pulled out his cell phone and opened the map app he had on it. "What's his address?"

"He ain't got one." Stanley giggled like a Southerner who thought he got the best of someone.

"What does he mean?" Bill looked from the young man to Burt.

"He's homeless. Has been ever since his wife was killed by a snake bite in Tanzania."

"Shit!" Bill sighed. "Where does he reside then?"

"He gets around. He never really settles down in one place." Burt scratched his beard. "Maybe my memory isn't too good at the moment."

"Are you bribing me, Groves?"

"No. No. I just can't seem to pinpoint the exact location he frequents the most at the moment." Reluctantly, Bill dug into his pocket and pulled out his thick wallet. He then handed the man a twenty-dollar bill.

"Jackson. Nice. Maybe throw a Grant in there too?"

Bill's face turned red. He then found a fifty bill and slapped it into Burt's greasy hand.

"All the same, I think we should introduce you. He's skittish, you see."

"You need seventy dollars to take me to see some bum?"

Burt let out a hearty laugh, "No. I need a Hamilton to take you to him. Boat fuel ain't cheap these days."

"How does your fuel come into play here?"

"Meet me at the harbor where they filmed that shark flick, and I'll tell you." Burt turned. "Let's go, kid. I'm sure that waitress you fancy thinks we stiffed the bill."

An hour later at Edgartown Harbor, Bill pulled the Chrysler through the entrance. He had a couple of calls to make prior. One to Peter Kemp of the Vineyard Gazette. The man had been hounding him for information about the case all morning and into the afternoon. Something about the rights of the public. Either way, he had informed the press that there had been a drowning, and an investigation was underway. Furthermore, the Sengekontacket Circle beach was closed, and no swimming was allowed. It was all very suspicious sounding, but it was the best he could come up with. The other call was to Vernon. He had asked the sheriff to accompany him. If things escalated, he wanted protection. He knew that Burt and Stanley would not provide any.

The police cruiser was parked between the main building and the docks. The thought of a tiger shark hanging dead and torn up made Bill's stomach churn. He looked around and saw Burt and Stanley standing by one of the slips. There was a small boat parked there. Vernon was with them, clearly trying to get information out of them but his agitated hand movements suggested Burt wanted more pay for his say. Bill got out and hurried over.

"So where is he?"

"He's at the lighthouse."

"I see." The mayor stopped a few feet in front of them. "I take it this dinghy is your boat?"

"Do you think I could haul a fuckin' tuna on this thing? Hell no! Fuel money is fuel money though. This dinky vessel belongs to Stanley here."

"Will it hold all of us?" Vernon looked it over.

"Stanley's going to stay behind. Otherwise, I'd say no," Burt chuckled.

"Then what are we waiting for. Let's meet this Mr. Desmond."

"After you." Burt gestured for the mayor to climb aboard.

He did so and the boat tilted to one side. Bill nearly fell over the side but managed to catch himself on the motor. He then looked back at Burt, face full of rage. Meanwhile, the captain belly laughed, barely able to catch his breath. "Yer father may have been around boats, but you sure haven't!"

"It's been a while," Bill snarled.

"Yeah, well. Don't worry. We'll get your sea legs working by the end of all this," Burt said as he and Vernon climbed aboard.

Bill went to sit down in the middle center of the boat.

"Nope!" Burt held his foot out and covered it. "You'll never be a seafaring man if you take a seat on this tiny thing. What's next? You'll want a lifejacket?"

"As a matter of fact, if you have one?"

"To the bow with ya!" he shouted as he started the engine.

Vernon took over the seat where Bill wanted to sit. The small boat then took off and chugged across the small canal. The speedboat soon pressed against the white sand beaches of the island. The trip took no more than a few minutes, but Bill wanted to upchuck his egg and cheese bagel over the portside. Bill took notice.

"Yer not only green on a boat but around the gills and on yer big dumb face!" he hollered with laughter.

The mayor wanted to swing a left hook across the man's jaw but thought better. Especially with the sheriff being there. Instead, he took a deep breath and sighed.

"Let's just get this over with."

Trudging up the beach, towards the lighthouse, Bill began to feel the ache in his calves. He was not used to hiking up hills, let alone with texture as rough as sand. He instantly regretted his choice of attire and lack of exercise. His fatigue showed clear as day as he was out of breath within minutes of the journey. He wanted to ask how much further but did not want the almighty captain to chastise him for it. It was too bad that he had already noticed.

"Take it easy on those home cooked meals."

"I don't bring home leftovers if that's what you're suggesting."

"What? You ain't married? What kind of politician ain't married?"

"I am married! I have kids who take the leftovers with them. I usually just snack on cheese and crackers until lunchtime!"

"Oh, that's right! Those big business meetings at the best seafood joints in town. Only the elite of the elite, huh?"

"You have a problem with authority figures besides yourself, huh?"

"Damn right I do! Everyone else is too soft these days. Too soft and too fuckin' greedy."

Bill was huffing and puffing now. “You just got almost two hundred bucks off me. Who are you to talk about greed?”

“I’d be lucky to make that in a few days sometimes.” Burt looked over his shoulder at him. “You probably make that in a few hours or less.”

“Quiet! Both of you!” Vernon held up his hand. He had been in front of them but was now taking a few steps back. “Is that him?”

He made his way over the hill and his face turned pale. The man did not look as he suspected. Rather he appeared to be quite dead. Mangled and torn in two. His innards looked dry as if they had been baking in the sun for days. His skin was white as a ghost and receding. It made his eyes bulge out his sockets.

“No doubt in my mind now, men,” Burt said coldly. “We’re dealing with a crocodile.”

CHAPTER TEN

Ageless.

It had rested long enough. Now time to burn off the additional fat it had consumed, the great predator swam through the pond. Its slender shape made it appear as if it were slithering. Only small ripples could be seen on the surface as it made its way towards one of the crevasses. Plunging down, it located its escape route. Things were different now though. There were no openings to get through. The bottom looked like a hairline fracture ran across it, spanning twenty yards. Something had blocked it off.

The creature did not show irritation as much as bewilderment. There were other ways of escaping. The process was longer and more unveiling of its presence. An overwhelming sense of self preservation did not factor in its survival. Consume, rest, repeat. Those were the factors that made up its existence. Survival was a priority but did not constrict its progress for those attributes.

Only one option remained. It had to make it to the surface and onto land. It searched around for another opening along the bottom, but it was all in vain. There was no other choice. It swam up and crawled ashore. Its massive body slid on the grass at first, but it managed to pick itself up and scurry across the land.

***

"Jesus H. Treyt!" Keith shouted at the top of his lungs in a drunken stupor. "Did you see the size of that thing?"

He turned but saw no one standing next to him. Kane was in his own house. He had forgotten he had been alone. Keith quickly ran across the field and towards his neighbor's estate. His adrenaline was high but movements clumsy. He nearly fell into the door before he could knock on it.

"Grant! You in there?" Keith banged feverishly on the wood.

"What is it? Sturges?" Kane could be heard slowly making his way from the kitchen.

"The creature! It's on the move again!"

Kane opened the door and saw his neighbor. Beads of sweat poured down his face and his exasperated look was punctuated by his eyes. They were deep in their sockets but wide with fright.

"Where?" Kane asked.

"I swear to ya. I swear on my mother's grave, on the holy bible. The damn thing crawled out of the pond. It's making its way on the land!"

"Are you pulling my leg?" Kane asked.

"No. I already told you! I swear! The thing's a monster. Fast too. It was there one minute then halfway across our property the next."

Reaching for his rifle, Kane looked at Keith. "Show me."

It was growing humid as the afternoon wore on. Keith had a case of alcohol sweats, and he profusely expelled the salty substance from every one of his pores. Kane, on the other hand, was used to the near unbearable weather for some this time of year. For him, it was his own personal Florida. He had never visited there but had relatives who told him about the extreme heat and moisture in the air. The bugs whizzed around his head, and he felt as if he were in the swamps or everglades. It was hot, but not unbearable.

Keith began to pant.

"What are we looking for?" he asked.

"Tracks."

"I thought it was hard enough climbing uphill to your farm. I don't know why I'm sweating so damn much," he stated.

Kane paid him no mind as he observed the ground around the pond.

"Where exactly did it come out?"

"Over here." Keith panted as he pointed over towards the north eastern side.

"That's right by the trail and Seaview Avenue," Kane gulped. "Beyond that is the open ocean."

The two men hurried over. To Kane's shock and surprise, there were indeed impressions on the ground. They looked deep, and wide.

"Damn, this thing must weigh at least a ton," Kane explained. "I'd say it's over twenty feet long if I were to guess. Again, at the very least."

"We have to get the sheriff out here."

"I already tried last time. No one listened."

"We're so close to the preserve. Call them. If there is a threat to their protected areas, I'm sure they'll get involved."

"Maybe." Kane hunched over and examined the tracks closer. "This creature was not that low to the ground. It didn't drag itself out of here."

"What are you saying?" Keith asked.

"You said it was fast. That tells me it's got powerful legs and that it was not hampered by its own weight. I'm starting to think we're dealing with something new here."

"Maybe a mutation?"

"That's a big word for you, Sturges."

"Shut it, you old fool! It's got to be some large crocodile or alligator."

"Yeah. I'd say something like that. Although much different at the same time."

Staring down at the tracks, Kane gripped his rifle tight.

"Do you have your phone on you?"

"No. Got rid of it a month ago. I couldn't figure the contraption out, let alone pay for the damn bill."

Kane closed his eyes and took a deep breath.

"Go back and get it. Call those nature preserve people. Tell them there's a threat in the preserve. Possibly a large crocodile."

"You're not going after that thing, are you?"

"If I have to. Right now, I need to warn people before it's too late."

***

It had sat for twenty-thousand years. A formation that guided where to start a swim race, Lover's Rock had been buried in 1973 due to an erosion control project. It had sat near Inkwell Beach where a creature whose species was older than it now roamed. It had made it undetected so far. Snaking around alleyways and crossing backyards, it was close to the ocean and had yet to been seen. A salty gust of warm air blew by its scaly hide. It could sense that it was getting drier despite the humidity.

With the sea close, it decided to rest for a brief time. There was no hurry. It had already settled on a patch of shrubbery that could act as shelter and shade. It moved slowly at first, it used its inner ear to detect vibrations. The heightened senses it used could detect even the faintest movement. Body close to the ground, it picked up faint pattering. Most likely small prey. It did not bother with the insignificant morsal and it hurried over towards the shrubbery.

***

Kane had made it two miles on foot. He was thankful that, despite his age, he had strong muscles and the motivation to keep at things. The tracks had been a bit tricky in spots. The ground was not as mushy in certain areas. He still managed to locate where the animal was headed, like some big game hunter in Africa. He was driven by curiosity but also fear. Whatever this thing was, it was big and dangerous.

He found himself on Nantucket Avenue. At the end was a continuation of Seaview, some land, and then the sea. Kane had crawled over a couple of fences and found that the creature had busted through some weaker sections of them. Kane crawled through an opening it had created.

Nearing one of the last houses, he saw another hole. It led to a decent-sized backyard. He could not see over into the property but, gaging by the perimeter and how far the barrier went out, it was about the length of quarter of a football field. He wasted no time and crawled through.

A horrible noise filled his ears. It came from his right. He pointed his rifle in the direction but was thankful he had quick reflexes. A Pitbull sat in its doghouse. The canine was ferocious but carried a whine in its tone. Almost as if something had scared it not too long ago. Kane knew what had been the cause and that he was close. He hurried across the yard.

"Hey! Stop!" a man's voice could be heard.

The farmer did not listen.

"I'm calling the police!"

"Good! You do that!" Kane shouted as he jogged across the property.

Finding another gaping hole, he got on his hands and knees and hurried through it. He was now on Seaview Avenue. Across the road, there was some straw-laden land and then the sea. Totally in the moment, he ran across the street. More loud noises filled his ears as he turned and saw a police cruiser pull up to him.

"Put the weapon on the ground and get on your hands and knees!" a voice called out over a speaker system.

Kane stopped in his tracks. Every urge told him to run after the predator. He fought them and got down on the ground. The weapon was off to the side.

Deputy Rosenthal got out and quickly spoke inaudible gibberish into his radio attached to his side. He then hurried over and kicked the rifle carefully out of the way.

"You guys sure act fast when it's not an emergency," Kane scowled.

"Put your hands behind your back, Grant."

"So, you know me by name now?" Kane laughed.

"Your buddy Keith called the nature preserve for Farm Pond. He told them about your little escapade."

"Fucking moron," he replied, directing it at Keith and the deputy. "You need to get the police out there. There's a monster crocodile on the loose."

"Right." Rosenthal clipped the cuffs around Kane's wrists. "I'm sure there's a shark out there eating tourists too."

He picked up Kane who could barely stand. Fatigue was starting to set in and his limbs felt weighed down as if they were tied to rocks.

"Let's go. You can explain yourself over at the station." Rosenthal picked up the rifle as he guided Kane over to his cruiser. He then put the farmer in the back and took the weapon with him and put it in the front passenger seat. He drove off. Neither man said a word to each other.

CHAPTER ELEVEN

Things had changed.

At first, Daniel Brightly had been ecstatic about visiting Martha's Vineyard and seeing an old friend again. Since their arrival though, there had been a cloud of sadness and fear looming over the island. First the morbid visit to the hospital and now a man running across Anthony Butler's backyard carrying a gun. It was becoming all a bit too much. He had indeed called the police but had been informed that the suspect had been apprehended not long after.

Sandra was in the living room with Joseph who was playing on his phone. She looked downright mortified by what had transpired over the last few hours. Their son was deep into a video he was watching. They could not tell if he was trying to cope with what happened or if he was just bored. Either way, it was going to be an interesting discussion at dinnertime. That much, they were sure.

A car could be heard pulling into the driveway. Daniel quickly hurried to the door and opened it. Anthony was there, getting out of his vintage 1950's car. Daniel was never good with cars but he liked the design of it. The doctor noticed and smiled.

"Like it?"

"The color's nice and the windows where the blind spots usually are is a nice touch."

Anthony nodded and then grew sullen. "I'm sorry for what happened back there. There are no words to describe the scene that transpired.

Especially not when there were children in the room."

"Anthony what's going on here?"

"Unfortunately, I've been left mostly in the dark for the time being," Anthony began. "All I know it some kids were killed over by the Sengekontacket Circle and their parents want answers. Understandably so. It was a horrible sight from what I've heard."

"Did anyone see what did it?"

"I don't know. I did hear that Mitch Tucker was present when the boys were taken. He might have seen something, but I can't say for sure."

Daniel scratched under his chin. He looked puzzled.

"Was it a shark, perhaps?"

"That's the only explanation I can think of. Still, why now? The timing is too perfect in my opinion."

"It's just a movie."

"Still quite a coincidence. It's almost as if someone put the thing in there to time it just right for the movie's fiftieth."

The two stood in silence, both pondering on what it could be and why.

"We had to call the police earlier," Sandra said as she appeared in the doorway.

"I heard. One of the dispatchers notified me."

"Who was he?" Daniel asked.

"I believe it was Kane Grant, but I wouldn't put it past being Keith Sturges. The latter is more impulsive. I couldn't see it being Grant unless he had a good reason."

"Maybe we should talk to him?" Daniel wondered.

"That would most likely be impossible at the moment. Right now, I presume, he's being interrogated back at the station. We probably won't be able to for a day or two."

Daniel shook his head slowly. "I still think we should call to see if we can. I might be able to help."

"I suggest we have a late lunch and rest on full stomachs. We can call when everything's settled down a bit and we're rested."

"What about the hospital?" Daniel asked him. "Shouldn't you be there with your patients?"

"My staff is full and capable of handling them for the time being. I've been at it for thirty-six hours straight. They know I need some time. I'm getting up there in age," he chuckled softly.

"Do you want me to prepare something?" Sandra offered.

"I haven't had a woman in my kitchen in years. That would be lovely. Thank you."

The three went back inside the house. Anthony turned and saw Joseph playing on his phone.

"Well, you've certainly grown!" he exclaimed. "You were up to my hips last time I saw you."

Joseph looked up, smiled, and then returned to his phone.

"Sorry. He gets absorbed in that damn thing sometimes."

"Don't they all these days?" Anthony laughed.

Lunch consisted of some cold cut sandwiches. Bologna, cheese, and lettuce made up most of the sandwiches besides Dan's, who preferred turkey. Joseph was content with either as was Anthony. The four ate in silence in the sunroom. Trays were laid out with everyone's respected dishes and drinks in various positions. It was almost uncomfortable but Sandra could not remember when they had last had a meal as a family. Certainly not in the past four months. Daniel had been busy with a project for his bachelor's degree in paleobiology. He came down when he could.

She had to commend him for his commitment to his family. Most scientists who were in his position treated their spouses and children like the plague when it came time to study. Not Dan. He was committed to being the best father and student he could be. It came all the more of a surprise when he was the first to ask a question.

"Did I ever tell you two how me and Mr. Butler met?"

"I don't think Jospeh knows but I do," Sandra smiled.

"Well, I can answer that," Anthony chuckled. "I was but a mere sixty-five at the time. He was doing research in the Bahamas, studying some long extinct fish whose bones were found near one of the local resorts where I was staying."

"It wasn't a fish nor was it extinct. I was studying whale migratory patterns," Daniel chuckled. "Maybe I should tell the story."

"Nonsense. I can remember."

"It wasn't even the Bahamas. It was Puerto Rico."

"If you insist." Anthony held his hands up in surrender.

"As the good doctor was saying," Daniel began. "There were signs of several species of whale traveling odd paths in the Caribbean. My theory was that something was spooking them. It had been disproved and blamed on the weather. Regardless, Mr. Butler here was one of the first to report on a beached whale in Honda Cove. Authorities speculated it got trapped and afraid."

"What really happened?" Jospeh wondered.

"My theory is similar but that it was not trapped. Rather it was scared into a corner."

"What could have scared a whale?"

"Not just any whale. A humpback. One of the largest species of mammal on the planet," Daniel continued. "Whatever had happened, a forty-eight-foot behemoth had come ashore right in front of Mr. Butler's vacation bungalow. I was called in along with a few other specialists in the field."

"Yeah?" Joseph pushed for the answer to his question.

"Like I said. The weather did influence it. The whale was removed from the premises before any real investigation could begin." Daniel smiled. "Doc here had a million questions for the scientists, but I was the only one not snooty enough to indulge him."

"You were pretty up your own keister. I will give you credit though. I did indeed have a lot of questions, and you were more patient than the rest of them."

"We've been in contact ever since," Daniel stated.

"I wonder what happened to the whale?"

Sandra chuckled. "It doesn't matter now."

"No, I mean, where was it taken?"

"Most likely used for chum." Anthony raised his glass of milk to his lips ready to take a sip.

"Ewww," Joseph said suddenly.

"Better than letting it sit there and become bloated. It's the circle of life," he replied and then drank.

The evening wore on and it soon began to grow dark. Daniel and Sandra brought Joseph to one of the guest rooms while they took the hammock out in the sunroom. Anthony was willing to pull out an old couch, but it was dusty and had some old stains from a cat he once had. Time rolled around to nine and then nine thirty. Joseph was fast asleep by the time the first growl would have been heard.

It had slept outside in the bushes. When its eyes opened, the full moon shone in them. Glistening over its nictating lens, it watched as the stars beamed high in the sky. It reminded it of a primal time. A world unknown to this one. A waterscape of flesh and teeth. Even the land was unsafe. The shoreline was easy pickings for creatures such as themselves that fed upon the oblivious animals, searching for liquid nourishment.

The memory was not of its own. Rather it was instinct that had evolved through its species for countless generations. Through this it recalled the act. To hunt.

Letting out a deep, reverberating growl, the creature pushed through the bushes, rustling the leaves and cracking the sticks beneath its clawed feet. It desired to scour. To feed again.

It was not long before it found new prey. The sight was a peculiar one with a barrier between itself and the targets. A thin metal kept it at bay only momentarily as it pressed its snout against the cooped-up critters and gained immediate access. As they scattered about, it looked for the best option to consume. There were a few huddling in the corner. They made chirping sounds, almost as if they were descendants of other species its own had encountered millions of years ago. Snapping wildly, it tore through them in seconds. Feathers and blood covered its snout as it chomped down feverishly.

The consumption of these birds was but a mere morsal. It needed larger prey to satiate its growing appetite. Pushing through the wire on the other side of the enclosure, it managed to escape. Then, with a hurried pace, it traipsed across the road and plunged into the water. A trail of feathers trailed behind it.

CHAPTER TWELVE

Psssk.

The sound of hissing could be heard as Berry Stockwell cracked his *Seagram's* bottle. The *Island Berry* flavor was addictive as this was his fourth one this night. Thankfully, they were a low alcohol level beverage that he could enjoy a bunch of and not get limp dick. It also helped that he was overweight and able to store more in him and not get that buzz. He had truly lucked out for tonight. Sitting next to him on the dock was a girl he had picked up at one of the eateries. She was a knockout compared to Berry. He was having trouble remembering her name, more attracted to her looks as he focused on them over everything else.

Sure, she was a little intoxicated, but he did not think it was enough to impair her judgement. She had even mentioned liking his chubby cheeks. Her fiery red hair and buxom chest really were amazing. Her wavy curls were mesmerizing as was her button nose and small mouth. She was a real cutie. She turned to him every so often and blushed. She took a few sips of her beverage and smiled nervously. Berry tried to play it off cool but was a nerd at heart. He loved Star Wars and all things science fiction. To him, this woman seemed like one of those untouchable Comic Con girls. Except, instead of a crazy, revealing costume, she was wearing a blue blouse and matching headband and dark blue jeans.

She looked at him again and smiled. It was hard to believe she was drawn to him. As far as Berry was concerned, it was going to be a good night. They were situated at the end of a dock, feet dangling over the water. The moon was full, and sky filled with stars. The glowing buildings behind them cast a blue haze in the sky. It was visible outside, enough to see that the woman was becoming tipsy.

This was not what Berry wanted their first date to be like. Was it even a date? Besides that, was she really even attracted to him? He thought about making a move but did not want to risk ridicule or laughter. He was not attractive in the slightest. Freckles covered a lot of his face, and his thin moustache was anything but impressive. Still, she saw something in him. What it was, he was not sure.

"Berry," she said softly, suddenly.

"Yeah?"

"I have something I need to tell you."

"Uh, yeah. Sure. What's up?"

"Well, I haven't been very up front with you."

"Oh?" His eyebrows arched.

"Yeah. See. I know you. Well, I remember you to say the least."

"I don't think we've met before tonight."

"Remember high school?" she started. "More specifically, high school prom?"

His face went pale. "I try not to."

"Well, that dance you did. The one trying to impress Krista Knowell?"

He did not respond.

"I felt bad that she laughed at you. I could not believe that one of my best friends could be such a jerk to someone. We haven't spoken since we fought over it shortly before graduation."

"You're Amber Stratford?"

She looked at him sheepishly. "Guilty."

Berry laughed. "I can't believe it."

"Sorry. I didn't mean to deceive you."

"No. No! It's okay. I'm happy that you said that. Truth be told, I heard about you and Krista's fight. I tried to find you in the halls but never did."

"I was all caught up with all my classes," Amber stated. "I just showed up to graduation and that was that."

"Damn. How did you find me?"

She smiled. "I may have stalked you for a while."

"Well, I'm glad you found me."

"Me too." She took his hand gently. "Wanna get out of here?"

Berry held up the *Seagram's* and noticed it was empty. "Let's make more memories."

He tossed it, waiting to hear the splash. It did make a noise but not the one he was expecting. They both noticed and turned to see the bottle had landed in the mouth of some hideous creature. The cavernous jaws spread wider as they charged out of the blackness of night. Both could only sit there in total shock. They had never seen anything such as this abomination before. The very sight could turn hair white from shock.

Terrible teeth clamped down onto Berry's legs. Amber's hand happened to be placed near his lap and was caught in the grip as well. The creature tugged hard and pulled Berry over the side while, simultaneously, knocking into Amber. They were both in the water now with the horror from the sea. Amber's hand was still stuck in the jaws; she was dragged down while Berry pounded on its snout.

In a desperate attempt to survive, Amber pulled her hand free, ripping skin and muscle as it went. The saltwater stung fiercely as she clutched her appendage. The webbing between her fingers was split all the way past her palm. It looked like it had been ripped in two. She looked around, the water stinging her eyes. There was no sign of Berry. She pushed herself to leave the depths, kicking wildly with her feet. A mere five feet separated her from the surface. Her lungs burned as did her hand. She could see the moon shimmering along the surface.

Something hard and painful slammed into her side. Teeth dug into her body around her chest and torso as the mighty monster dove with her again. She screamed in pain. Once she could no more, she tried to breathe in but water filled her lungs. Before she could slip into complete unconsciousness, the behemoth swung her around like a ragdoll. She came apart in two halves. It swallowed one and went back for the other.

The attack had been so swift. As stealthy as the creature had been at first, the act of taking its prey was a bit abrasive. There were no signs of people on the beach. No one walking the boardwalk. The area had an eerie calm about it, a stillness in the night. It was no wonder then when it took those two on the dock that it had gone undetected. Blood had settled on the surface amongst the calm waves. It was as if none of it ever happened.

It was not without witnesses though.

Over on Seaview Avenue, pressing against a railing and donning a pair of binoculars, Keith Sturges saw the whole thing. He had been keeping tabs on the creature as it swam through the inky black water. The bright moon cast its light onto it. It plowed through the waves but was clearly low enough to not make too much of a commotion. He did not see the poor couple on the dock until it was too late. It had made a wide turn and then darted right for them. Before he could scream for them to get out of there, it was too late. His attempted aid was squandered when it took the first bite.

All Keith could do was watch in absolute horror as it chomped down on them. It tore the chubby man off the docks and knocked the rather beautiful woman into the sea. She seemed to have been stuck in its jaws too. When they both went down, neither resurfaced. He was now hyperventilating. He had to make it to the police station, but he did not have a car. He felt around for his phone.

"Shit!"

He could not believe he had forgotten it again. Instead of hoofing it towards town, he spun around and ran as fast as he could back to the farm. It would not be a short journey. He had not realized how far he had come. Even with the attack being far away, he was still a good forty-five minutes or so from his estate. His labored breathing began almost immediately. His sprint turned into an exasperated jog. He was both annoyed and frustrated at his out-of-shape body. Soon, his speed slowed to a walk. Then he stopped entirely and leaned over, pressing his hands above his knees and began to try and catch his breath.

Each throaty gasp for air was deep, almost choking. It was accompanied by a similar sound, though more akin to a growl. It started and stopped many times as if it were hyperventilating or running. Keith pushed off himself and turned to see the creature. It was about fifty yards out, barreling straight for him down the road.

"Fuck!" he exclaimed and then turned to run.

His legs would not take him far. They felt like cinderblocks weighted down with rope. Each step he took, he could feel the straining and hear the creaking in his bones. He decided the best bet would be to hide. There were only two options. One was the grass to his right. The other was a field on his left. There was no option. He began to think logically as fear drove a spike into his mind. The idea of discovering his body to aid in the investigation occurred to him. He then gave up the fleeing prey angle and turned around.

"Do your worst." He grinned but then noticed the animal was gone. Completely out of view. It was like it had vanished or had never been there at all. Keith gave a loud sigh.

"Goddamn booze! You are really starting to get on my…"

Before he could finish it came from the left. It had done the same thing as when it attacked those two on the dock, making a wide turn to finish the job. Plowing into Keith, it nudged him over towards the sea. Before they got there, it pinned him down. Staring at him with sinister, flaming yellow eyes, the creature then scooped him up and began to swallow. Keith tried to fight it by pounding his fist into it wherever he could.

"No. No. No!" He could only watch helplessly as the bright night sky disappeared, and he entered a new kind of blackness.

Within less than a minute he was down the animal's gullet and swallowed whole. The man was large enough that he could not move much in the tight space that its stomach held him in. Soon, the cries stopped as he had presumably run out of oxygen. The creature then hurried back towards the farm area. It was time to rest again.

CHAPTER THIRTEEN

Reporting.

Peter Kemp had grown tired of Martha's Vineyard. His loathsome response to the lackluster claims was shown in not only his work but public reputation. He was a man of suave nature once. He could charm the pants off any beauty pageant contestant on the island. That was a time ago. Back when his profession literally did not care about the minor stories. Drunkard locals and ballsy tourists. It was brutal this time of year and he was in charge of it all.

Now there was a drowning. Big whoop. What intrigued him most was that the mayor called to inform him of the occurrence. It was not unlike him to do so but the exchange was anything but leisurely. He had spouted so-called facts to him and then hung up, obviously in a hurry. A rush was more like it. The big man was running around trying to cover up loose ends. Bill was a loser, but Peter liked having him in his back pocket. It helped to have connections.

Smoke permeated his car. It was a little nitpick none of his lady friends liked. Still, he made an effort to cover it up with car fresheners. The effect it had was minimum, like spraying axe body spray on a man with bad B.O. It just made it worse. He decided to roll down the window and let in some of the salty air. He was near the farmland and figured the earthy odor pallet would do wonders. What met his nostrils instead was wretched. Like someone cut up a cow and then set it on fire. He gagged immediately.

"What in the otherworldly hell?"

As he drove by the Grant/Sturges estate, the smell became utterly fowl. He could not really see over the hedges, but Peter was willing to bet money that the pungent putrid pile was coming from one of the herd's own. The land was vast, and it could have wafted down from somewhere further on the property. Thoughts of carcasses filled his mind. It was not his land though and Grant was known to be friendly with his rifle. Peter did not need a broken window or blown out headlights. He kept on down the path that eventually took him to Seaview Avenue.

The morning sky was a hazy blue. The contrast of misty dew and greyish hues brought about a light fog that blanketed the road. It was making it hard for Peter to see more than a few feet in front of him. He slowed his vehicle and kept an eye out for any idiots who decided to go for a walk in the thickness of off-white. Then, out of curiosity, he rolled down his window again.

If anyone wants to call me out for shitty driving, then they'll get my lecture on the ethics of walking in weather like this, Peter thought to himself as the window began to crack open. The same smell hit him again. It felt akin to being slapped in the face with a moldy raw steak.

"What the hell is that?"

Thud ump. Thud ump.

There was the noise and vibration as something rolled under his tires.

"Son of a bitch! Now what?" He slowed the car even more.

Swinging his arm over the seat, he strained his neck to look out the back window. The fog was so thick that it was nearly impossible to see anything. Just a wall of cloudy white. Contemplating what to do next, the outside odor was becoming more pungent. It was becoming difficult to breathe. Finally, he brought his vehicle to a complete stop. He did not want to get out and take a look around. The atmosphere around him reminded him of old British horror films from the sixties. The only thing he needed now was to run into a mythological monster of old cinema. Slowly, he opened the door and stepped outside. He was surprised to find the air was thin and the temperature warm. He should have known given it was summer and condensation but the icy feeling he got from his surroundings warped his sense of logic.

He fished out his phone and quickly pressed the flashlight app. It was dim and barely had any effect. Yet there was something beyond the light that shone. It was not far from him, perhaps a good ten yards. He had not realized how slow he had been driving or how far ahead he had stopped. It was clear now that the distance he traveled was very little from when he had run over whatever it was that now lay before him. He took a few steps, unable to draw the beam from the object. He would not dare to do such a thing. Part of him thought that, if he did, it would close the gap between them. It would be some malicious figure, filled with teeth and waiting to satiate its hearty appetite. As he got closer, he realized it was not a creature nor was it even alive. His grave expression turned sour. It was a pair of binoculars. A shadow, cast by the flashlight, gave them the impression that they were a large figure.

Unaware that he had been holding his breath the whole time, he exhaled. He knelt forward and examined them. The glass within was clearly shattered and the black casing was smushed as if it were plastic. They looked like a cheap throwaway pair anyway. The very idea that they were out in the middle of the road was odd.

Then he noticed something that made him pale. Surrounding the optical equipment were dark droplets that covered the ground. It was as if a crimson substance had splattered all over the ground. He then held his breath again. The grim reality of the situation made several scenarios play out in his head.

It couldn't be a joke. Not much laughter for a reaction you couldn't see in this fog. Murder? Unlikely. Where was the body? Why does it look like the blood sprayed everywhere on the ground instead of it having pooled into a puddle? The only thing that made sense was that someone was attacked by an animal. Most likely eaten. He hurried back to his car and drove off. As he did, he requested his phone to make a phone call through Bluetooth.

"Call Mayor."

The command was repeated back by an anatomical voice for confirmation which Peter gave. It rang a few times before a groggy voice picked up.

"This'd better be good," Bill's voice came through Peter's speaker system.

"I've got another *drowning* victim here." The emphasis on Peter's sarcasm on the word drowning was unmistakable.

"Who?"

"I don't know. I found a pair of binoculars and strangely dispersed blood. It looked like someone was attacked by a fucking lion," Peter explained.

"Where?" it was all that Bill could ask.

"Seaview Avenue. Get someone out here. Lot of strange happenings on this side of the island. Wouldn't you agree?"

Peter could practically see Bill nodding on the other end of the line.

"I think you and I need to have a talk."

"When?"

"Meet me at my house in an hour. There are some things that need to be discussed."

It was a fifteen-minute drive to Boldwater Road. In that time, Peter contemplated on how to brace himself for whatever news Bill would tell him. Before he pulled up to the luxurious property, he came to a stop at a gate where he was given access to pass by a burley man wearing a suit that was a size too small. Peter became nervous.

"Really pushing security around here, huh?" he had asked the guard who gave him back his credentials, license and reporter identification.

The man only gave a half smirk and then went into the control house. He pushed a button that opened the gate and Peter passed through, waving him off.

Once inside the estate, he noticed the yard was just a clean plane of grass. There were no bushes or fountains. Nothing that told of the mayor's wealth. It was nicely kempt and a lush green but, other than that, it was rather barren save for one statue. It was near the set of old oak wooden doors off to the left. It looked like a snake coiled around a tree. As Peter got closer, he realized it was one of a hideous dragon type creature wrapped around a weapon, a spear of some kind.

Bill came outside and met the reporter next to his parked car. It was a bit odd seeing as how the place seemed to be locked tight. The man seemed to feel most safe in here.

"Hello, Mr. Owen," Peter said as he got out of the vehicle.

"Bill, please. I told you. No formalities," he replied while shaking the reporter's hand vigorously.

Peter nodded. "Security seems to be more present than before."

"Yes. Well. With the way politics are now, one can never be too careful."

"I can see that," Peter said, his eyes wandering over towards the statue again.

"Oh!" Bill exclaimed. "I see you've met Vannessa!"

"Vannessa? You mean like the myth?" Peter's eyebrow arched.

"Yes. Someone gave me that when I first moved here. A real striking piece, wouldn't you say?" Bill seemed overly enthusiastic, as if he was eager to show off his property to anyone.

"I'd say so."

"Come! Let's get inside. There's much to discuss." Bill ushered the reporter inside who watched the statue intently the whole way in.

Once inside, Peter was taken aback by the interior design. There were carvings in the ceiling. Great battles took place in still images right above their heads. Peter was no expert in ancient history. Yet the chariots charging towards fleeing soldiers presented to him that it was of Greek origins.

"Quite the place you've got here."

"Thank you," Bill continued. "I appreciate your call. It was most disturbing but unfathomably important."

Peter took note of just how much the mayor's demeanor had changed since their talk over the phone. His mannerisms and entire attitude were of suave intellect and high-class presentation. It was interesting, to say the least.

They soon made their way into the den where the embers of a once roaring fire were dying down. Now all that remained were the crackling sounds of the wood and the hints of orange coloring on the logs where the flames dwelled. Peter examined the room further. He was drawn to several paintings. Bloody battles were played out as if motionlessly acting out the real-life warfare. Spears were driven into chests and swords penetrated flesh. Morbid yet fascinating.

"So. About this lion." Bill turned to Peter.

"I didn't say it was a lion. It looked like something attacked someone like a lion would."

"Ah, yes."

"Also, there were no tracks because it was on cement. I don't know what actually happened or what caused the mess," Peter stated.

Bill walked over and grabbed a fire poker and began prodding the pit. "I don't think there are many predators like that around here. At least, not on land."

"What? So, a shark got him? If you tell me that and I publish it, we'll be the laughing stock of the town!"

"I don't want you to publish anything on the matter, Mr. Kemp," Bill's tone was changing again.

"I have to do something. This whole thing's got me shakin'. I wouldn't feel right if we did nothing," Peter explained.

"You have nothing to worry about. We'll have it sorted out soon. In the meantime, push for publicity for the island. We need tourists to still come even though the beaches are closed. Try to make an article on our lifestyles or the history of Martha's Vineyard."

"No one will read it."

"They would if there was a missing person article on the front page, if you catch my drift." Bill stood up.

Peter nodded. "If I don't run with that story and something else happens, I will disown ever being involved in whatever little scandal you have going on here."

"I don't want a panic, Mr. Kemp. I want this island to thrive and keep the safety amongst the people."

The reporter scoffed. "As you wish."

"That'll be all." Bill turned to him and shook his hand. He then escorted the man outside and watched him as he drove away. Once he passed the gate, he peeled off down the road.

CHAPTER FOURTEEN

A halt in the plan.

Joseph Brightly did not know why his father wanted to cancel the Jaws location tour at such short notice, but he would never let him live it down if he did. That much he did know. His dad had been pacing around Anthony Butler's living room all morning while he sat there brooding on the old, dusty couch. It was getting annoying and there was nothing anyone could do about it. His mother knew that the previous day's events were still stuck in the man's head but there was little to go against. She felt the same way.

Sandra still held onto the idea that maybe taking him on the tour would be good for them and that it would be a nice way to get their minds off the tragic scene that befell them less than twenty-four hours ago. She sat watching as the sun peeked over the horizon. Despite the doctor's house being a relic straight out of the 1980s, she had to admit one thing that was very apparent. His house had a great view of the sea beyond the yard. Occasionally, she saw the dog in its little house poke its head out. Something had spooked it greatly.

She had seen Anthony walking over to try and call the canine out of the doghouse, but he had little luck. As the sun rose higher, he began to look like he was snooping around. His investigation caused his whole demeanor to change. No longer was he relaxed and caring towards the pooch. Instead, he was on edge. He was looking over the fence that surrounded his property. He was mainly focused on an area that was close to his pet. He looked concerned and even somewhat appalled. Then he looked at the grass as if something had left a track or trail in the yard. He followed it and that's when Sandra noticed the gaping hole on the other side of the property.

"Oh my God," she said softly.

The tone of her voice made Daniel snap into action. He ran to her side and looked out the window.

"What is it?"

"I think you were right. Something did come through the back yard last night."

Daniel examined the lawn. The sun was high enough now to cast light over the entire area. There were indeed strange markings and broken fences on either side. Beyond that, the dog was still cowering in the safety of his little home.

"I'll be right back in," Daniel spoke gravely.

He hurried outside and met up with the doctor who was examining the gaping hole on the left side of the fence.

"What is going on here?" Daniel asked.

"It looks like some kind of animal charged through here."

The marine biologist looked down at the ground. There were tracks but the body itself was low to the ground. They looked reptilian, as if some amphibious monstrosity charged through the backyard. He placed his hand over one of them. The imprint was a few inches deep.

"What was it?"

"Crocodile, maybe. I'm guessing a big one too."

"How big?"

"Let's just say I'm surprised it didn't take the entire fence with it."

"That big, huh?" Anthony scoffed. "Great. Just what we need during our busiest season."

"I'm afraid it may be worse than that."

"What do you mean?" The doctor's eyebrow arched.

"It didn't go after your dog," Daniel stated.

He responded with a single laugh. "So?"

"That means it probably already ate when it was crossing your property. Or it was hunting something or someone else. A bigger game."

"So, in other words, we're in deep shit?"

"I'd say we should get the police out here."

"I'll call them. I don't think they'd listen to you. No offence but you are just a visitor on this island."

"None taken. I already called them last night about the trespasser on your property."

"Why didn't you tell me?" Anthony exclaimed.

"We were all asleep by the time you got home," Daniel explained. "Besides, they said they already apprehended the guy. Although, I'm starting to think he was on to something."

"Or hunting something," Anthony added as he came over and stood next to Dan.

They both looked at the trail and tracks as if a hideous revelation came to fruition. Yet they were still clueless as to what was going on. It made them feel helpless. Daniel looked up at the window. Joseph and Sandra were sitting by it. His son looked annoyed, but Sandra shared the same concern.

"Regardless, I don't think you should cancel the Jaws tour you booked for your son. I doubt a crocodile would travel that far from the sea. Besides, the beaches are closed. I think it should be alright," Anthony told his friend.

"I hope you're right." Daniel smiled for the first time all morning. It was directed at his family. Joseph immediately responded to it and grinned. Both of their expressions told of the same thing. The tour was on.

***

Despite the beaches being closed, the vacationers flocked to the island. Whether by ferry or private plane, people were coming in droves. Tourists in their own right, many had been there before. They would be treated as such despite their worth. Curtesy was a different story. If they tipped in hundred-dollar bills for every little thing, most guides would be enthusiastic. It was not only a good time for the business but commercialism as well.

Morgan Tucker watched as a smaller boat pulled into one of the slicks. The sun was beating down on the island and, therefore, Burt Groves was sweating like a hog caught in a sweltering heatwave. Stanley Reed was doing better but it was clear he was the harder worker of the two. He was perspiring a bit but he was in much better shape than his captain. Morgan did not know them that well, rather he knew of them. Namely Burt. A true capitalist. He still had common sense but was not above throwing a lot into a little. He recalled a time he walked by when the filthy captain bet against his mate that he could catch a fish before him. It was five bucks but he still succeeded because his line hit the water first in a section of the dock where it was a given you could hook a scup.

Stanley placed down a toolbox and looked up. He recognized Morgan right away and waved. The tour guide returned the gesture.

"Got any guests you taking around the island today?" Stanley asked.

"I'm booked up. Today's the fiftieth anniversary. It's going to be crazy," he replied.

"Well, if you get any isles who want to go fishing, give us a mention, will ya?" Burt added.

"I didn't know you were in the chartering business?" Morgan said.

"Always up for somethin' new. Besides, the bitin' has been shit 'round here."

"Yeah," Morgan said softly. He didn't know if he should tell them about what he saw. That pair of long, reptilian jaws snapping around that kid. Half the island thought he was hallucinating. The other half thought he was crazy for still doing tours the day after.

"Well. We'd better get back to work." Burt nodded to Stanley who groaned.

Morgan forced an awkward smile. "I'll leave you to it."

As he walked away, he could hear the two bickering over the tasks that had to be completed before the heat got even worse.

Out somewhere in the harbor, another ferry's horn blared. More guests were arriving. Morgan looked at his watch. It was quarter of nine. He had fifteen minutes before his first customers arrived. He shook his head at the thought of what he was doing being immoral. It was a business. The kids being eaten was separate, but he could not dismiss the fact that the beaches were closed and no one else would be hurt. Those visions of them being plucked under the surface would haunt him for the rest of his days. He had seen some horrible accidents in his life, that one took the cake.

As he made his way over towards his van, he saw a family of three standing by it. The father, he presumed, waved him over. Morgan came over and smiled.

"Are you my nine o' clocks?"

"Yes."

"Okay. We're going to have a full bus today so, if you don't mind waiting, they should be here any minute," Morgan explained.

"Okay. No problem," he continued. "My name is Dan. This is my family. My wife Sandra, and our son, the massive Jaws fan, Joseph."

Morgan smiled at them all. "Nice to meet ya."

"Are the beaches really closed?" Joseph asked.

"For the time being, yes," Morgan sad, sullenly.

"Aw, that means I can't jump off the bridge."

The thought of another kid being eaten by the monster triggered Morgan. He would not let it happen again. For their sake and his. He had heard the parents' reaction was understandably unsettling. He had not seen Buckley or his grandson since the accident. Last he heard they skedaddled from the island. It was also a reasonable reaction. He tried to maintain his composure and took a deep breath.

"Unfortunately, that is true. We can drive across the bridge though."

"Can I go on the rocks?" Joseph wondered.

"I don't know." Morgan rubbed the back of his head with his hand. "We'll have to see when the time comes."

Daniel wanted to side with the tour guide. Part of him figured he knew way more than he did. The gravity of the situation was great. There was a predator out there. Crocodile or not, something busted through the fence as well as killed a bunch of kids by the bridge. If this man thought it was safe, he would take his word for it. He was not sure if Sandra would though but time would tell.

"Oh great!" a familiar voice called out.

Dan's decent mood turned dour when he saw McGrew and his family walking up the hill towards the van.

"Honey, don't start a scene. For the kids' sake," his wife pleaded.

He nodded but never took his eyes off the marine biologist.

Morgan pretended not to notice the hostility and waved them over. "You must be the McGrew family."

"Yes," the father replied.

"Alright!" Morgan clapped his hands together to liven up the vibe. "Let's get this tour underway!"

CHAPTER FIFTEEN

Passage.

With its high metabolism, the body parts flowed through the creature's body with ease. Along with that, its constant need to move burned calories faster than it could intake. It had been in the crevasse for a long period of time. Now, it was free and constantly swimming. It was a wonderful feeling as water brushed against its scaly skin. Like hearing a babbling brook, it sensed that the warm liquid ran over it with a gentleness that could not be mimicked. It felt at peace until its stomach groaned.

The time had come. With a low growl that reverberated under the water, it pushed itself off the pond floor. There was barely a ripple as it surfaced. It gracefully swam towards the shore. It did not feel eyes on it, nor did it feel in danger, hunted. Rather, there it was free to make its way across the farmland and towards the road. Past that was the sea.

Suddenly, a new feeling came over it. It was as if it were reinvigorated to kill. A passion came over it like no other. It had experienced it before. Only when it desired to consume. Impulsively, it scampered across the grass and soon found itself on the barren road. It crossed another stretch and plunged into the ocean.

***

Vernon Hackery was law on the island. There was no doubt about that. Yet he felt he was losing. Whether it was the fact that he had not stopped the threat or that his office had been getting calls about sharks in the area. Sharks were not his problem. That much he knew. The public did not though, and fish fever was taking over people's rationality. There needed to be something held accountable for those kids' deaths. Now there were reports of a couple missing, last seen around Seaview Avenue.

The sheriff rubbed his temple as he watched a group of young teenagers pass by. The inkling that they could be the next victims of whatever was out there was not lost on him. Worse yet, they looked bored and liable to do something stupid like breaking a certain law put in place about the beaches being closed.

"You kids need help with anything?" he called out to them.

Some of the girls giggled while one of the boys smiled and shook his head.

Yep. Up to no good.

Although he could not arrest them for simply walking around. He was not a crooked cop but, in this instance, he wished he could.

Soon, they were out of sight and Vernon looked around. The throngs of people were coming in from several ferries parked alongside the docks. They looked eager yet wore a look of disappointment. Probably because of the beach closed sign that greeted them from across the walkway. Some shook their heads while others flipped off the sign as if it felt any real despair at their gesture.

"Fucking tourists," Vernon whispered under his breath.

"What's that, Sheriff?" Deputy Rosenthal asked.

The lawman forgot he was standing right next to him.

"Nothing," Vernon continued. "Where's Rigmond? I want him out here too."

"He's back at the station," Rosenthal replied.

"Why the hell is he there?"

"Remember? Kane Grant is in custody."

"He's not going anywhere! I want Rigmond *here. Now*!" Vernon shouted a little louder than he intended. Some of the tourists looked over at them. He tried to reassure them everything was fine with a smile. Most fell for it, but others continued to stare. He reached for his walkie, ignoring them.

***

Katlyn could not believe her mother let her go off on her own. She was fourteen and ready to live life. Somehow, she sensed that her parents knew this and had different reactions about it. She was an islander year-round but had always been guarded by her overbearing father. He was like her shadow, watching over her, by her side every step of the way. By some miracle, he had been called in to work at the restaurant. He was head chef and two of his employees had called out "sick". Her father had added the quotations as he spoke to her mother.

She had promised him that she would not let their daughter out of sight. That was the way it was until Casey came to the door. She was tom boyish yet still very pretty. She had asked if Katlyn were at home and if they could go to the boardwalk together. It was a good cover story they had hatched over text. Katlyn's mother prodded her with questions, but Casey managed to keep her head and the story straight. Almost slipping a couple of times yet she never broke character.

After all that, it had worked. Now they were with Chad and Trey. They were all around the same age. Chad was the ringleader, given he was the oldest at age sixteen. Katlyn informed them all that they were not to go to the Crab Shack near the boardwalk. If her father found out they were out and with boys, she would never hear the end of it. It would be a legendary stern talking, to say the least.

"What was that cop's deal?" Trey asked, trying to play up his Boston accent.

"Hell, if I know," Chad nailed his pitch perfectly. "Pig probably sniffed our plan out."

They all chuckled.

"Why can't we just go out to eat or to an arcade or something?" Casey wondered. "What if a shark is really killing people?"

"You're paranoid," Chad laughed. "That or you've seen Jaws too many times."

"I'm so sick of hearing about that damn movie," Katlyn groaned.

Chad began to hum the theme song like a creep. He motioned towards Katlyn who moved away. They kept at it, quickly building up speed until they were running. The boy made a chomping motion with his arms in a wide arch.

"Watch out! The shark's gonna get ya!" Trey yelled out, cheerfully.

The two ran down the street until they were near the boardwalk. Katlyn stopped dead in her tracks. Her father was outside having a cigarette. Chad did not seem to notice so she acted quick and moved around the back. He followed, not knowing he was being lured away from prying eyes.

Katlyn soon stopped near a dumpster. Chad did too and began to catch his breath.

"Did I scare ya?" he asked.

"No, dipshit! This is where my father works!"

"Really?" Chad looked around. "Oh yeah! I didn't even realize. I'm sorry."

"It's alright," she giggled.

"Does he ever come back here?"

One of her eyebrows arched. "Not usually. The other employees do though. Why?"

"Well. I was kind of wondering if you'd like to, you know?" He paused.

"No? I don't." She shook her head slowly.

"Well. Let's just say I've seen the way you've been watching me."

"I haven't been watching you!" she said defensively.

"Hey! It's all good. No harm, no foul!"

They stood there in awkward silence. Katlyn looked around the alleyway as she thought about her father. He never let her do anything fun. At least, not when he was around which was always. Why couldn't he let her enjoy herself? Now, here she was, with her secret crush, which was not apparently a secret, and she was feeling free for once in her life.

"Come on. Trey and Casey are probably looking for us."

"Let 'em." She grabbed a head full of his long straight hair that went down over the side of his ears and almost to his shoulder blades. Holding him close, she planted a kiss on his available lips. Chad was taken aback at first but then leaned into her. They began to grope each other when they both stopped. A noise was coming from below them. The alleyway rested right over the water. They could hear the lapping of the waves brushing against the pilings.

"What was that?" Katlyn wondered.

"Maybe it's a shark! A great white!" Chad laughed heartily.

Just then, the whole backway shook. Something was indeed smashing around down there.

"It's probably a piece of driftwood or some shit," Chad tried to reassure her, but it had little effect.

"Maybe we should get back to them."

In that moment, Chad snapped at her. "Why are you girls always so skittish? You playing hard to get or something?"

"No!" She stood her ground. "I just think we shouldn't be back here. Maybe we can find a nice spot on the beach and then…"

Before she could continue, someone came through the back door. Katlyn froze as she saw her father standing there with a look of shock and then anger. He then turned to Chad who was already backing away.

"Chad Myers, get away from my restaurant!"

The kid wasted no time taking off. Her father then turned to face her.

"There's something below us," she stated.

"Come inside! I'm calling your mother!"

Reluctantly, she followed him inside. Her begrudging attitude sparked an idea in her father's head.

"Maybe we'll have you do some chores around the restaurant on top of being grounded."

Katlyn feared if she looked up at her father, he would be wearing an insidious smile. Perhaps he would start laughing at her and her failed attempt to live a free life. She could only look straight ahead as they walked inside through the kitchen, and towards his office. The restaurant was not that big which was why her father could have it sitting right at the edge where the road met the dock. Even if it were spacious, she would still feel claustrophobic. She sat down in the musky room and began to reach for her phone.

Her father pulled it from her grasp so easily it was as if her hands were covered in soap. He then placed it in one of the pull out drawers at his desk and locked it inside.

"Dad!" she exclaimed.

"What!" he shouted at her. "You have no say in the matter."

"I'm not five anymore!"

Instead of his usual response which would entail her to stop acting like she was younger, he reached into his pocket and fished out his own phone. He then began to dial.

"Please don't call Mom! She had no idea!" Katlyn pleaded.

Giving her a half-smirk as if he enjoyed the torturous reaction she had to finding out her mother was getting in trouble too, he waited for the phone to pick up. When it did, a deep voice came over the line.

"What do you want, Gerald?"

"I need a favor."

"Why would you call me when I called out sick?"

"Well, you see, my daughter offered to pick up a shift because you were unavailable. I was wondering if you could stop by and bring her your uniform?"

"You don't have any more?"

"Sorry. I have to order some."

There was a sigh on the other end followed by, *"Fine."*

"Thanks, Todd. Oh. Before I forget." Her father turned to her with a creepy smile that she was unsure how to take. "Don't forget your apron."

***

They sat on the beach under the bridge. As small waves brushed against the shore, Trey and Casey lay there. Each incoming push and pull of water felt magical. They giggled, not only at the sensation of the sea carefully coming over them, but their lips pressing together. There was a time and place they planned to announce their relationship. It was clear no one had any idea. Not even Chad or Katlyn, their own parents, or anyone at school.

Casey had a hard time containing herself around him. He was always Chad's groupie. With his tacky Hawaiian shirts and wavy sandy blonde hair, he was her own dream boy. Every time he smiled her whole world lit up. His face was smooth, and skin, tan and shiny. His almond brown eyes called to her every time they looked in her direction. He was the exact opposite of Chad who could be douchey at times. Trey had a sweet side that most never saw.

In turn, Trey was enamored with her. She was unlike any other girl in school. She wore jean overalls and always kept her baseball cap backwards. She had braided pig tails that ran down the length of her back. A petite little thing she was and yet she would stand toe to toe with the bigger girls and even some of the guys in their class. Her dark pupils seemed to fill her eyes, and her eyelashes were long. When she was happy, she always seemed cheerful. Yet it was clear there was an edge to her.

Another wave was coming and, this time, Trey unbuttoned one of the flaps on her overalls.

"Not here!" she giggled.

"Why not? No one will see us. Or hear us for that matter."

"I've got a better idea." She quickly got up. "Come on!"

He too stood up and followed her. They made their way towards one of the pilings further in and she pressed him against it. They could feel the ocean flowing by and hear it causing vibrations in the wood. They kissed for what seemed like an eternity. Then, she began to lower herself.

"Oh shit!" Trey said in amazement as she began to reach down and slide her hand in his khaki shorts.

Something growled and it was not his stomach.

Looking up, she saw a pair of glowing yellow eyes. They were almost dark enough to be orange orbs hidden in the darker regions under the dock. It was off to their right, whatever it was. She froze in fear and Trey noticed immediately.

"What's the matter?" he asked, genuinely concerned.

She did not answer. Instead, her lower lip began to tremble.

"What's wrong?" he asked again.

Taking a step back, she was clearly afraid of something.

Trey took note of this and looked in the direction she was staring at. There. Hidden over by the beginning of the dock, there was something there straight out of a nightmare. It looked serpentine with a long scaly body. It even slithered a bit as it moved. Yet it was not a snake. It began to walk towards them on all fours. The bipedal horror was unlike either kid had ever seen. It was huge, gargantuan even. It reminded Trey of a dinosaur like out of one of those monster movies he spent time watching as a kid.

"Let's go," he said softly.

Casey was almost out from below the docks. Trey was slowly catching up to her. Neither took their eyes away from the living, breathing terror. No matter how far they made it out, the creature was closing the distance faster. Trey noticed this.

"Run!" he screamed.

His plea snapped Casey out of it enough to make her turn half-hearted back walk into a sprint. Trey did too, but was not fast enough. The creature took a massive lunge forward and snapped down around his legs. Casey looked over her shoulder as she ran and stopped.

"No!" she cried out as her secret boyfriend was torn apart right before her eyes.

By the time the jaws crushed his stomach and blood spilled down his red and white Hawaiian shirt, he was dead. He hung backwards and then flopped up and down as it chewed and consumed his body. Soon, it had him in its stomach. The hideous horror had pretty much swallowed him whole.

"Trey! Casey!"

A familiar voice called out to them. Unaware that she was the only one alive. It snapped her out of it and she looked up at the docks. Chad was looking down at her.

"What's going on? Where's Trey?"

"Mu. Mu mo. Mo Mon."

"What? Speak up. I can't hear you!"

"Monster!"

"Nice try. You guys better not be fooling around or something. Katyln and I got caught. Best to keep a low profile for now. Get me?"

She did not respond.

"What's the deal?" Chad asked.

She almost looked like a ragdoll being pulled back into the docks the way she had been. It happened so fast that Chad's mind could barely compute what was happening. Casey was there one minute and then frothing water that soon turned red came next. It took longer than normal for Chad to realize a giant pair of crocodilian-like jaws had grabbed her and was now tearing her apart. When he did, his whole face turned pale. He took two steps back and bumped into a tourist.

"Watch it, man."

They took notice of how petrified Chad looked and reluctantly stopped.

"What's the matter? You on drugs or something?"

"It's down there," Chad said softly.

"What? Aw, man. I ain't got time for this. I have to get to the tour bus."

"It killed them."

"What killed who? A shark eat someone or somethin'?"

Chad's mind had snapped. He was not sure what he saw anymore. All he could recall was the blood. Unknowingly, he nodded.

CHAPTER SIXTEEN

They wanted blood.

A frenzy occurred down below the dock. It was not a school of fish swarming a chunk of bait or people feverishly splashing each other to have some summertime fun. Rather it was the antithesis to both. It was not amazing or cheerful. Several lawmen and a couple of reporters were making their way under the boardwalk. They frantically searched for signs of life. All they found were limbs.

Vernon Hackery was beside himself. He had been too busy scolding Deputy Rigmond for not being there when, all the while, the creature had killed again. Now it was gone and all that remained in the aftermath was blood and body parts. Rosenthal was growing nauseous while Rigmond was starting to lose his cool head. Deputies Hex and Foster were not doing great either. Their skin was turning a sickly green and white. The only one who seemed unfazed was one of the reporters. Peter Kemp had always wanted a big story. Now he was getting one.

The whole debacle was going to be a disaster once news spread of a killer crocodile. The worst part was that it was a shark, according to the witness, that had grabbed his friends. Though another individual insisted he nodded when he spoke of a giant great white. Vernon was not sure if he spoke the truth but he was the first one to run into the kid and call the police.

Sharks and crocodiles, Vernon thought as he shook his head. *What's next? Rampaging eels? Mutant snakes? Sea scorpions?*

"Over here!" Hex called out.

The group of five headed over to him. He looked as though he was ready to turn in for the day and spend the next week in bed.

"Whatchya got, Hex?" Vernon asked.

"I think it was resting here," the deputy explained.

Examining the spot, it was dark even with the flashlights. There were still indications that something was there. The water was low enough that the sand did not fill in too fast. There was an indent about three and a half feet across.

"Why would a shark be resting near the shore?" Peter asked.

"It could have just been a log, or the sand could have caved in in that area." Rosenthal suggested.

"I'd believe the latter," Vernon stated. "Best back away in case of it sinking further."

Everyone did as the sheriff instructed.

"I think we've got everything we need," Foster suggested.

"Forensics will have to scope out the rest of the area when they get here," Vernon stated.

The two reporters were already making their way onto the beach, both occasionally glancing over their shoulders as they went. Rigmond walked over to the sheriff.

"Why did you let them come over?"

"I want to make one thing clear," Vernon snapped at him. "This was some maniac. There is no shark out there."

"What are you talking about?" the deputy wondered.

"If we start saying it was a shark, it'll be open season on all fish and whales in the area. I don't want a public outcry over this."

"What about the chief? Is he onboard for this? He already thinks you're going behind his back," Rigmond said.

"The chief won't even make his way outside for an afternoon walk. Let alone hunt for a killer. I've got this. I don't need him slowing me or the progress of this case down."

"What about those kids near the bridge, or that missing couple? What about the dead diver that apparently drowned despite being an expert in the water?"

Vernon rubbed his temple. "I think it's time we talk to the mayor."

As if on cue, Rosenthal hurried over to them with the big man in tow.

"Mayor's here, Sheriff."

"I can see that. Go do crowd control with Hex and Foster. Lord knows everyone wants to see some blood."

Rosenthal cocked his head but then hurried up towards the beach.

"This is a P.R. nightmare!" Bill cried out.

"Please, sir. Be calm. I think I can solve this."

"Really? What? Some murderer is slashing people on the beach. Lord help you if that's your cover story."

"Well. Actually," Vernon wanted to continue but fought the urge.

"I'm calling Chief McKenzie. We're putting an end to this once and for all."

It took ten minutes too long for McKenzie to get down there. The usual minute drive was hampered by what he claimed was traffic and the hustling crowd over by Oak Bluff's fishing pier. Already the mayor was in front of the bridge's entry point with Deputy Rigmond on his left and the sheriff on his right. The mayor must have been making some grand speech because his hand gestures were waving wildly out of control.

Sitting on a bench next to them, facing away from the crowd, were two fishermen. It was not a huge area so finding a place to sit was heaven sent as far as

McKenzie was concerned. He continued to push through the throng of people and waddled over to the three men. Three other deputies were keeping the pushing crowd back. Even Peter Kemp was trying to get front and center. Everyone had so many questions and the chief felt not only out of his element but oblivious to the happenings in his own jurisdiction. Confronting Vernon face to face, he stared at him with seething eyes. Vernon knew he was in a world of hurt after this was all said and done. McKenzie then took his position next to him.

"Thank you for joining us, Chief McKenzie," Bill stated.

"I wish it could be under better circumstances," he said loudly.

"As I was saying," the mayor continued. "The past twenty-four to thirty-six hours have been a horrible time for this island. I can't express my sincere apologies enough to the families that lost those kids on the beach. The police department are investigating the missing couple as we speak. However, I speak for the department when I say that there is more going on here than meets the eye."

A bead of sweat drizzled down the side of his face in all sorts of random directions until it landed on his suit. It was not only clearly hot in that attire, but he was choking under the pressure of it all. Vernon was about to step in to intervene when the mayor continued again.

"While, yes the kids were attacked by some large predator, it has been discovered that it washed up on shore over in Farm Pond by one of the caretakers there."

Vernon did a double take towards the mayor. He had not been informed about this whatsoever. For the first time, he felt as in the dark as the chief.

"It was retrieved and brought to a biologist to study on the mainland."

"What was it?" Peter jumped at the first opportunity to ask that question.

"It was a shark!" several voices shouted.

"It's karma for that movie being made here!" another called out. "After all the harm it caused those fish, one has come back to seek vengeance."

Trying to pick through the crowd to see who was making such a bold statement, the mayor gave up after a few seconds.

"If it makes you feel better it was not a shark."

"Bullshit! That kid said it was!" the same voice called out.

"What's your name, sir?" the mayor inquired.

"My name is Buckley! My grandson was almost killed by it over on the Jaws Bridge yesterday! I sent him home but stayed to see this thing through."

"The problem has already been handled. There are more pressing matters at hand!" Bill exclaimed.The crowd went silent.

Bill gave a sideways glance and almost rolled his eyes but knew it would break the illusion. "Reports of a maniac have surfaced. This individual slaughtered those kids below that dock. If there is any involvement between them and the missing couple, I promise you it will be dealt with swiftly."

"Again! Bullshit!" Buckley laughed this time.

"It was no shark!" a voice from the officials' side piped up.

Turning to the bench, one of the fishermen got up. "It weren't no shark. Nor was it no goddamned man."

"Keep out of this, Burt." Vernon took a step forward.

"Burt. If you don't keep in check, I'll have you and Stanley there arrested," Bill snarled.

Burt scoffed. "Fer what?"

"Disrupting the peace." Vernon took another step.

The crowd watched with intensity as the scene played out before them. Though it was not Burt nor Stanley who was disrupting the peace. Rather something scaly and slimy that was making its way out of the sea on four stubby legs that caught everyone's attention.

"What the fuck is that?" Stanley suddenly screamed at the top of his lungs.

Chief McKenzie was the first to see it out of the other lawmen. It seemed to slither along but was a bipedal creature. It rammed into Deputy Rigmond, jaws snapping wildly around his midsection. The creature's body slammed into the mayor and sent him sprawling over Vernon and the chief.

Everyone got out of its way as it chowed down on the local lawman. Hex, Foster, and Rosenthal withdrew their service pistols and fired at the abomination of nature. The very same monstrosity whipped its head back in response and swung the now dead Rigmond around, sending him skidding across the road. A trail of blood and flesh lined the way.

Wasting no time, the deputies continued to fire. Blood exploded in some spots of the creature's body while others bounced off its scaly hide. It whipped its tail at Hex and sent him flying into a nearby telephone pole wire. Becoming entangled, he was electrified. His skin quickly searing and turning an inky, burnt black.

Peter took pictures like a madman. He was getting close but kept a safe enough distance, or so he thought. With incredible speed, the animal bopped him with its snout, and he fell onto the hard ground. His camera smashed into hundreds of fragmented pieces, but he paid it no mind. Instead, he got to his feet faster than ever before and ran.

"Get everyone out of here!" Vernon shouted as he pushed the mayor off of him. He then looked down and saw the chief was unresponsive. Flipping him over, he saw his head bleeding profusely next to a decent-sized rock. He looked around for anything to stop it. Without a first aid kit or cell phone in sight, he dug for his own.

The call did not take long, and he managed to get hold of Anthony Butler as well. The way the day was shaping up, it was going to be more hell than ever thought before. Vernon then looked over at Bill. Both men knew they were at fault. Now they had to deal with it.

Meanwhile, Burt and Stanley had quickly made their way down to their parked truck. Stanley turned back and saw the chaos unfolding and then looked at his captain.

"There's nothing we can do, boy."

Stanley wasted no time, opened the glove box, and reached for the pistol Burt had stowed in there. He then turned and ran.

"Where are you going?"

"Someone's got to do something!" Stanley shouted over his shoulder.

CHAPTER SEVENTEEN

No one could have predicted.

As the tour van passed over the *Jaws Bridge*, everyone was visibly disappointed. With the beaches closed, the absence of kids playing in the water and nearby beaches made it seem void of life. Even Morgan himself found it to be eerie. Normally every time he took this route, there was a sense of cheeriness despite the disturbing scene in the movie having taken place in the exact location. Not only that but seeing those kids get mauled himself made him glance down at the water. The thought of a pair of hideous, crocodilian jaws appearing from the gloom made the hairs on his arms stand up stiff. It was awful. The way the boy reached for him and how helpless he was. Morgan was unable to save him.

There had to be a way to undo the mental image. To wrong the rights. He did not understand why it happened. No one did. It was just nature taking its course. It did not make it any less horrifying of an experience. The teeth. The screaming. The blood.

He was starting to think it was not such a good idea to continue the touring after all. There were other ways to make profit off the tourists, but this seemed like blood money. He was deep in thought when he was thrust forward. He did not get a chance to cry out when it happened again. One of the tourists' kids were slamming their feet into the back of his chair. Attempting to tell the parent to get control of their kid, he failed when his chair was kicked again.

Daniel took notice of one of the McGrew kids who had become unreasonably bored and began to pound his sketcher sneakered feet into the cushioned seat. He too wanted to tell him to stop but held his tongue. That is until the child began to cry out. If it was one thing he could not stand, it was spoiled screams from a rotten child.

"Jessup! Knock it off!" Mr. McGrew shouted.

"But I'm bored!" the boy of eleven whined.

"We'll be getting out of the van soon to get something to eat. I promise," his mother told him.

Sandra looked at Daniel, both equally irritated.

Thankfully, Joseph seemed to be absorbed in the scenery. He was consciously aware of the annoying brat but did not let him disrupt the scenic view of Martha's Vineyard. It was a picturesque island with plenty of color between the locations and locals. Morgan seemed nice but, other than that, he had not met any other islanders. The view was similar to what it had been fifty years ago. White sand beaches, grassy dunes, tranquil water. It was all the more of a shock when he saw the monster charging for the van.

"What is that?" Joseph shouted.

The boy kicking the seat stopped and grabbed hold of the head piece on the chair and pulled himself up. "Is that a dinosaur?"

Morgan had time to recover but not enough for his mind to process what he was seeing. The leviathan reptilian menace was chasing several locals and tourists around the town. Some of them were charging for the water as if it would do them any good. It did not follow though. Instead, it exerted itself as it narrowed down on a young man shooting at it with a rifle.

It was Stanley.

"Holy shit!" Mr. McGrew cried out.

Daniel could only stare in amazement. He was in the middle row but could see it clearly. The creature was large. Well over twenty feet long. It looked like a crocodile but with a slimmer body tone and rougher skin. The scales were smaller too. They covered its blueish-grey body. The yellow eyes looked like large pieces of ember with a black circle in the middle. It took the marine biologist all of fifteen seconds to realize what it actually was.

"My God," he gasped "It's a Nothosaurus."

"A what?" Mr. McGrew asked with almost a humorous tone.

"An aquatic reptile from the Triassic Period. They were active from 210 to 240 million years ago! Their remains were found in North Africa, Europe, and China!"

"Looks like it's alive and far from home, buddy!" Mr. McGrew scoffed.

"It's that thing!" Morgan cried out in utter horror. "It's that thing that killed those kids!"

The creature stormed towards Stanley who was standing his ground. He took several shots while a nearby reporter did the same but with his camera instead of a rifle. One bullet grazed right above its eye, slicing through the arch around it. It roared out in pain and then turned its attention towards a fast-approaching vehicle. It seemed to home in on it like a missile, targeting to destroy. The great predator charged past Stanley who got another shot off. This one hit it on its back. A plum of red mist exploded. It left behind an addition to the collection of scars on its body.

"Holy Shit!" Mr. McGrew exclaimed. "I think that thing is coming right for us."

Morgan had not entirely realized that he was still going at a decent speed. He had been too wrapped up in the physical return of a manifested nightmare. He released his foot from the accelerator and slammed on the brakes. Everyone lurched forward. The annoying kid slammed against his chair hard.

"Hey! Watch what you're doing!" Mrs. McGrew shouted.

Ignoring the plea, Morgan put the car in reverse and began to back up. Before he could get too far, the creature had gained speed and was quickly closing the gap between them. For the first time since seeing the animal, Morgan looked over his shoulder. Thankfully not a moment too soon as another car was coming up behind them. He could not tell if they were driving or if he was just getting closer. He had to hit the brakes again.

The car behind them began to back up as well. Morgan's pleading eyes would not be seen by the driver but the horror in front of him would. When the car was a few yards away, he began to drive in reverse again.

"Oh, man!" Daniel said suddenly.

In no time, the creature smashed into the van and was now climbing atop the hood. Morgan honked the horn in a desperate attempt to scare it. The action did not seem to phase it. If anything, it seemed more driven to attack. The tour guide then put the car in forward drive and punched it. Surprisingly this worked. The creature did not seem to weigh as much as he thought it would. He drove as it snapped its jagged-toothed jaws wildly at the hood of the vehicle.

All the children were screaming. Mr. McGrew was losing his mind. He began to bark orders to Morgan while screaming like a madman that the thing was going to kill them. Daniel was the only level-headed person in the car at the current moment. He was observing the creature out the window; it seemed to be testing the hood for weaknesses while smashing into it. There was something both fascinating and terrifying about it at the same time.

After having driven a whole, terror-filled minute the car began to slow. The added weight was taking its toll on the vehicle. With the animal shaking around it caused the van to lose mobility and it was buckling under it all.

"Right before it breaks through, get out!" Daniel ordered them.

"Are you insane?" Mr. McGrew laughed manically.

"If we stay in here, we'll be sardines for the creature. At least it'll have to climb out before it can attempt to get us."

"Where do we go?"

Morgan looked to his right. "There's a summer cottage over there. It's our best bet!"

The vehicle then came to a complete halt. Smashing through the roof feverishly, the Nothosaurus' teeth started to pierce through the metal.

"Oh my God." Sandra began to think of a prayer but was too terrified to remember them from her youth.

A chunk from above came out. Then another. Its teeth made a terrible screeching sound as they dug into the ceiling above, their last bit of coverage.

"When?" Mr. McGrew screamed.

Daniel did not answer. Instead, he waited for the timing to be perfect. It had done as he had hoped. The animal was breaking through the middle of the vehicle. It came smashing down again; this time, a long portion of its jaws broke through.

"Now!" the marine biologist shouted.

They opened the single door on the side of the van. Joseph quickly hopped out but turned to wait for his parents.

"Just go!" Sandra yelled.

Joseph's legs refused to move at first. The van began to shake wildly as the creature dug around inside. Its jaws barely able to part yet still posing a supreme threat. He finally turned and ran for the cottage.

Sandra and Daniel got out next followed by Morgan who was able to open his side of the front door. He then pushed his seat forward and grabbed the annoying little McGrew boy as well as his siblings. Mr. McGrew was trying to get his overweight wife to move but she was hyperventilating badly.

"C'mon, Helen!" he exclaimed.

"I can't do this, Duncan!" she screamed while looking at her husband with pleading eyes.

"Yes, you can, woman!" He grabbed her by the shoulder.

She let out a blood curdling scream and began to wave her arms around frantically. Duncan felt at a loss. She was losing it and he was unsure what to do. She began to cry. Her pudgy face covered in streams of tears. Duncan began to inch for her again. Panicking, she swiped his hand away.

"Let's go!"

"I'm going to die!" Her face went pale.

"No. Honey!" Metal creaked above her head as the creature's jaws began to widen the gap. They were able to marginally open and close now.

Out of nowhere, Daniel came up to them. He stood beside Duncan.

"Mrs. McGrew. Please. Don't do this. Your children need you. So does your husband." Snapping out of her brief trance, she looked over towards the condo. By the entrance was Sandra along with Joseph and three other young, scared faces.

"Don't leave them." Daniel looked at her with wide eyes.

Shimmying out of the slow-crushing van, becoming free of fearful entanglement, Helen moved. With the aid of both Duncan and Daniel, they got her out. The creature's jaws were still trapped and, in turn, so was it. The three of them hurried over with a decent pace. Duncan constantly looked over his shoulder. The distance was not far enough as far as he was concerned. Daniel watched as Morgan opened the door and ushered Sandra and the children inside.

"Hurry!" he shouted.

With an excessively brash cracking sound, the Nothosaurus broke free. It snapped wildly in the air as if to make up for lost attempts. It then looked over and narrowed its eyes on the trio running for the building. It climbed off the destroyed van with ease and sat there.

"The damn thing's giving us a head start!" Duncan cried out.

Daniel looked over his shoulder and noticed it eyeing them like a dog being told to wait for its treats. All it needed to do now was lick its chops. It was very unconventional behavior for any reptile. Most modern-day species of archosaurs such as crocodiles grabbed their prey while the getting was good. Here, the creature seemed to be mocking their progress.

"Let's get a move on!" Daniel suggested with urgency.

Another shot rang out. This time, it was one of the deputies. It struck the creature under its armpit causing a gush of blood to spout forth. It turned and snarled at the man who quickly took aim again. He fired and fired, presumably, hopefully keeping track of the amount of ammunition he had left. His Glock 17 Model had already used at least eight of his cartridges. There was no way of telling how many he used before.

The creature roared at the officer. It was deafening, reminding Daniel of a blaring horn as if from a lighthouse.

Making their way through the entrance, Morgan watched as the deputy fired two more rounds until his Glock ran dry. He did not turn to run but rather reached into his vest pocket for another mag. Morgan realized if he could get it he would have seventeen more rounds to defend himself with. It was all the more disheartening that the creature was abnormally fast, quickly snatching the lawman and shaking him to and fro. Blood splattered onto the ground by its feet. It chomped once, ending the man's life and causing a pool of red plasma to build on the cement street below. Morgan looked away and shut the door.

CHAPTER EIGHTEEN

The horror he knew.

Kane Grant hunkered down in the prison. After Rigmond left there was no one to talk to. Not that no one could hear him. Two cops were on regular patrol checking in on him and some other fellow in the cell next to him. He kept singing obnoxious sea shanties. Both officers were growing annoyed with him but insisted he remained where he was. The farmer lay on the bed and covered his ears as an only means of blocking out the drunkard sailor's chants.

He still could not get over the fact that some large monster was out there and no one was believing him. Sure, he tried to explain it to not only Vernon, who looked a bit worse for wear, but he had gone out of his way to tell every cop of the menace out there. They grew as sick and tired of it as much as they were the fisherman's sea shanties. They were becoming saltier and more egregious, talking about women and feeling them up.

If Kane could spit far enough, he would do so at the man. His choice of topics were not only appalling, but so was his body odor. It was a mixture of a lack of deodorant and poor hygiene. He reeked more than any man Kane had ever encountered. When he shifted on the top bunk, Kane wanted to gag. It was a pungent odor brought about by disregard of one's own self aroma.

The only means of escape was to focus on his thoughts. The very idea that something so out-of-this-world was roaming around Martha's Vineyard was troublesome. The where and why were what drove him. Where did it come from? Why was it here? How did something so abnormal come into existence? At first glance of its tracks he thought it was a crocodile. Now, after chasing it, he was not so sure.

"Attention all units!" Vernon's voice came on over the radio of one of the guards. *"I need you to report to Oak Bluff. Over by the Flying Seahorse Cottage. There's been an attack. Hex and Foster are dead. Chief is injured. Ambulance is on the way. Multiple casualties."*

The guardsman picked up the radio and informed the sheriff that he was on his way.

"What's happening?" Kane shouted.

"I'll tell ya what's happenin'. It's them damn aliens. They've come for us," the fisherman laughed.

The officer paid no mind to the ramblings of the man who was already continuing his shanties, except now they talked about flying saucers and anal probing. Instead, he quickly rushed out of the hallway.

"Damn police never listen." Kane shook his head. "They don't know the horror they're about to face."

"Yeah. It's not your problem though," his cell neighbor stated. "They don't know their assholes from their elbows. As far as I'm concerned, they'll get what's coming to them."

"I can't just sit back and let it happen" Kane gripped the bars and shook them furiously. "There has to be a way out of here."

"Sure! Just let me produce the key from my keychain," he laughed wildly.

Just then, the door to the hallway opened. A man came running in with one of the office desk workers trailing behind. She looked agitated. It was as if she had been told to let him in against her will. It became all the clearer when the man began to reach for his pocket. He pulled out a ring of keys and a pistol.

"What the hell is going on?" Kane shouted.

"Man, am I glad to see you, Burt!" the fisherman cheered.

"You owe me big time for this, Wilton!" Burt replied.

As he attempted to find the right key, Kane watched with bated breath. Perhaps there was one on there that could get him out as well. Finally, Burt inserted one and they all heard a click. Wilton wasted no time in sliding the gate open.

"Do you have one there for me?" Kane begged.

Burt looked him over and tossed them his way. They landed inside by his feet.

"You owe me one too," Burt told him and then grabbed the desk worker by the shoulder and guided her outside.

Once Kane was out, he hurried outside after them. He did not want to get in a vehicle with his smelly cell mate, but he was not about to steal a police car either. He saw that the two men were already backing up out of the parking spot. Waving his hands frantically, he managed to catch the man he heard named Burt's eye.

"Stop!" he cried out.

Burt rolled the window down. "We don't have time for your slow ass, paps."

"I may be old but I chased that creature down last night. I kept a pretty damned good pace."

Wilton scoffed.

"We're not going after it," Burt stated. "We're going as far inland as we can."

"We need to help those people!" Kane pleaded. "I heard over the radio that there were multiple casualties."

"I already lost one crewmember to the call of aid. I ain't going to lose a fellow fisherman on my watch again."

"Stanley dead?" Wilton looked in his direction.

Burt gulped. "He went to go play hero. As far as I'm concerned, the creature got 'im."

'So, yer just assumin'?"

"It's better to assume than be in that thing's gullet!" Burt seethed with tension and impatience. "We're leaving. We let the authorities handle it."

"Two were already killed!" Kane exclaimed. "How many more people have to die because of this thing before you come to your senses?"

"Don't talk to me about coming to my senses!" Burt said, threateningly.

Kane walked in front of the truck. "Or what?"

Hands tightening around the steering wheel, Burt stared down at the older man. They both shared a distinct hatred for the creature but for very different reasons.

"Don't push me, old timer," Burt continued. "Don't you dare. I'm not afraid to knock some sense into you. I'll kick your ass so far in the past you'll forget the day you were born."

Wilton looked over to Burt from the front passenger side. "Calm down, Groves."

"No!" Burt shouted. "If you two want to go play hero, then get the fuck out of my truck. As for me, I'm heading inland and hunkering down until all this blows over."

"Let him!" Kane laughed. "He already left, what was his name, Steven to die. He obviously has no problem saving his own ass at the expense of others."

"His name's Stanley." Burt's face turned red.

"You remember that." Kane pointed a finger at him. "You remember the man you knew who you let die in the jaws of that thing!"

Wilton then unexpectedly undid his seatbelt, opened the door, and got out.

"Where you goin'?" Burt glared at him as he made his way over to Kane.

"I may be a son of a bitch. But I'm no coward."

Kane tried not to gag as Wilton stood next to him. Despite his honor and the respect he had earned from Kane, there was no denying he reeked. Instead, he stared at Burt for a few seconds and then turned and walked away. Wilton followed.

"That's what I get for breaking you out of jail, trying to save your smelly ass?"

"They would have let me out after I sobered up," Wilton called over his shoulder.

Burt watched as they made their way out of the parking lot. It was going to be around ten minutes before they were where that abomination against nature would be. They were going in unprepared yet ready to help. All he had to do was drive the other way. The island was just that, a mass of land surrounded by water. If he could get far enough inland, he would be safe. That did not stop him from continuing to stare at them. He pulled down the visor to block his view. A feeble attempt. He looked at himself in the mirror.

How could I live with myself? he wondered. *The hell with them! They chose to go after it. They're no better than Stanley.*

He tried to force himself to begin driving. Anywhere but there would do. No matter how hard he tried though, he could not lift his foot off the brake pedal.

"Shit!" he snarled.

As Kane and Wilton became smaller and smaller objects the further they went, the dilemma intensified. Burt began slapping the wheel of his old beat-up truck. He found himself uncontrollably driving forward. He made it as far as one of the exits. Looking one way, he saw a road that led to safety. The other, to chaos and carnage.

After another minute, he decided.

CHAPTER NINETEEN

Blaring like a foghorn.

The Nothosaurus bellowed a sound not too dissimilar to the lighthouse alarm that echoed across harbors. It was a nightmarish noise that made tourists and citizens alike close their windows and lock their doors. Its feet slapped against the hot pavement with each slimy step. Lower jaw parting only slightly, it seemed to be inviting everyone inside. It would mean instant death. Small birds had landed on its snout in the past to feed on barnacles or their own catches from elsewhere. Here, there would be a reasonable meal to attack if anyone dared to come close.

Daniel watched with utter fascination as it made its way off the street and into the lot of the Flying Seahorse's front yard. It trampled over the small shrubs without any indication that it felt the prickly pines brushed against its greyish blue skin. The eyes were haunting as they darted left and right, searching for new prey. They narrowed on a few options, but they were ultimately too far to engage.

Duncan McGrew and Morgan came to his side simultaneously. Both wore a look of concern. Sandra and Helen kept the children close. They were afraid but felt they were safe inside so far as the creature did not see them. It couldn't see them, could it? The very thought began to cause Helen to form horrible images inside her head.

What ifs and hows plagued her mind. What if it broke in and, if it did, how would it dispatch them? There was a service desk over by the elevators, she observed. *Perhaps there's a weapon or a way to call for more help.*

Sandra noticed she was looking rather faint and offered to have her sit down on one of the couches in the lounge. She nodded and walked away.

"What are we going to do?" Duncan wondered.

"We're going to wait it out," Daniel explained. "It knows we're here. The damn thing's scoping out the area for the easiest and most accessible prey. It's acting strange. Somehow, I don't think it'll come in here though."

"Why do you say that?" Morgan looked to him intensely.

"Because it's passed the door twice now."

"Maybe it's just looking for another way in," Morgan spoke grimly.

Helen continued to make her way over towards the couch until Sandra was not watching her anymore. She then hobbled over towards the check-in. The area had two computers, a bunch of buttons underneath, and two phones, one on the right side of each monitor. She began to feel helpless, useless. That was until she spotted a red switch on the wall. *It's our only chance,* her own voice told her in her head.

"I think it's giving up!" Duncan cheered somewhere in the background.

Helen did not pay him any attention. That thing would never give up. It would hunt them down until they were dead. Until all their children were dead. She was not about to let that happen.

"I think we're in the clear," Daniel spoke with optimism that was cut off by a sudden alarm.

Beeeeep. Beeeeep.

White lights flashed along the ceiling. Morgan was quick to realize what had happened.

"Who pulled the fire alarm?" he shouted.

"We need firefighters if there are no police!" Helen called out to him over the incident sound.

"You dumb bitch!" Duncan was past the point of not swearing in front of the children. "Do you know what you've done? You literally just rang the dinner bell for that creature!"

Helen looked upset with herself and then horrified. Behind the three men, the creature came careening through the doors. Morgan and Daniel jumped out of the way. Duncan was still directly in its path.

"No!" Helen cried out.

Duncan, who was now sat down on the floor while covering his head and ears, did not hear his wife scream. Nor did he hear the creature's rapid approach. The only thing that was somewhat audible was the alarm.

"Get out of the way, Dad!" Jessup McGrew screamed in a high-pitched girly voice.

Before he could react, the ceiling above began to buckle. It showed signs of cracks racing across. Fixtures snapped and lightbulbs popped as rubble came down on them. More and more damaged chunks came crashing down atop the Nothosaurus until, all at once, a huge slab of concrete collapsed atop it.

Stanley ran over with Rosenthal tagging along. The reporter, who was fascinated by the young man's bravery, was not far behind. The whole entranceway was blocked off by rubble. There were sounds of screaming on the other side.

"Let's get them out of there!" Stanley ordered the deputy.

"Right!"

The two began picking up sections of debris at a time. A plume of smoke escaped from one of the busted pipes and it shot out between them. The reporter had thankfully remained on the left side where Stanley was. He snapped away with his camera as if the two were suddenly firefighters rescuing people trapped inside a collapsed building.

"All you two need are some hard hats, huh?" the reporter chuckled.

Rosenthal turned towards him. "Put that thing down and help us!"

"This is a thousand-dollar camera with national news inside. There's no way I'm relinquishing it."

"Forget him," Stanley said. "I think we're almost through anyway."

Removing a chunk of concrete with small sections of rebar attached to it, they finally found life. It was not the kind they were expecting. It was the creature's tail. Swinging frantically, it was clearly still alive and agitated. "Step back!" Rosenthal instructed the two civilians.

The length of the creature slowly came further and further out as it backed up. Rosenthal and Stanley pointed their own pistols at it while the reporter used his camera.

"When its head is clear, open fire!" Rosenthal ordered.

With a swift whip of its girthy appendage, Rosenthal was sent flying back into a signpost. The reporter took a few steps back as it emerged. It came out so fast that, before Stanley could get a shot off, it nudged him with its snout. He tripped over his own feet and landed in the pavement behind him. Turning to its left, the pair of crocodile-like jaws, lined with jagged teeth, accompanied by hideous breath, bit down on Rosenthal's leg and severed it in one clean chomp.

"Ahhh!" the deputy cried out.

Instinctively, he reached down for his sidearm. It was a few feet behind him. He rolled over and began to crawl on his stomach. He did not make it far. Instead of eviscerating him, it scooped him up and began to swallow. Rosenthal screamed as he descended the creature's abnormally large gullet. One of his hands managed to find a gap between the teeth where he held on for dear life. The animal's tongue continued to roll back, pulling him further in.

"Help me!" he screamed at the reporter who continued to witness the world through his lens.

He began to lose his grip.

"No! No! No! NOOO!"

A puff of red spray erupted above the creature's teeth. Then another and another. Rosenthal looked and saw Stanley charging with his pistol, firing wildly.

The pain in the deputy's leg was severe and he could feel his own blood pooling around the corner pocket of the creature's mouth. His stump was splashing around in it. He cried out, rather shrieked, in abject horror as it turned with him still in its jaws towards Stanley.

"Just shoot it!" Rosenthal begged. "End it!"

Stanley stopped in his tracks. It seemed as if everything was moving in slow motion. The animal's massive head swung side to side as blood poured out of its jaws like red drool. He did not want to look at the sight of this insidious animal but managed to force himself to so he could take aim. Judging by the way the cranium moved, he figured he could get a few pops off between the eyes in one of its mid-swings.

It should have been expected but Stanley did not factor it as an option. The creature stopped waving its prey around and tilted its head back. As it did so, its tongue worked overtime in loosening Rosenthal like a kernel in one's teeth. The only shot he had now was to shoot under its chin. He positioned his shot but stopped. He did not want it to puncture through and hit Rosenthal. At this point it may have been a favor.

There was no more time to ponder on it. He took the shots. The first one hit right at the tip of thc underside of its mouth, the other strayed off.

"You're shooting too high!" the reporter called to him.

"No shit!" Stanley aimed again.

It was too late.

Rosenthal disappeared down into the creature. He would reach the stomach soon enough where he would burn alive in its stomach acid.

"Damnit!" Stanley cursed at the creature.

"Just like that. Hold it!" the reporter told him as he took a picture of the fisherman, mid scream.

"What is wrong with you?"

"I've seen enough here. I'll make you a front-page star!" he said, ignoring his question.

"Get out of here!" At first, the reporter thought the fisherman was telling that to him in anger. It was another emotion. One of fear and terror.

A sudden shadow was cast over him. He looked up and saw the massive tail coming down at him. The reporter did what any good journalist/cameraman would do. He shrunk back and clutched the camera to his chest.

Splat.

Crawling away, the creature dragged its tail along the ground, essentially grinding the reporter's remains into the pavement.

Stanley watched as it marched back towards the sea. He raised his pistol and pulled the trigger.

Click.

Empty.

CHAPTER TWENTY

Picking up the pieces.

There were many fingers pointed but none seemed to make any sense. The mayor had tried to warn people and close the beaches. Things took an unexpected turn. The law had been on his side and now four deputies were dead and the chief in critical condition. Burt, despite his cowardice, had tried to help as much as he knew how. There was no one to blame and, therefore, Oak Bluff became a source of morbid turmoil as they waited for the beast to return.

Now the only questions that remained were how and why.

Morgan and the tourists had found a way out through a back exit. Despite some scrapes and bruises, they were unscathed. Mental stability was another matter. Helen McGrew had to be carted off by ambulance. Her sanity was slipping, and she had begun to regress to a child-like innocence. Nearly being killed once was enough to drive anyone mad. She had almost been responsible for her own husband's death, and it deeply affected her, resorting her to mumbles.

Jessup turned to his father. "Is Mommy going to be alright?"

"She's tough. We just have to be equally tough for her." He looked down at his son to reassure him, but his face was deeply devastated, shown by a temporary noticeable scowl and watery eyes. Then, his other four children came over to him and they all embraced in a group hug. When they broke apart, he spotted Daniel making his way over to the tour van with Morgan and a doctor.

"Go wait by the Uber car. I'll be there in a minute."

The oldest sibling ushered Jessup and his sister over towards the vehicle. They kept glancing over their shoulders to see what their father was going to do.

"Look at this!" he could hear Daniel say as he examined the damage to the van. "The thing must not weigh a ton but it's huge. It's definitely a Nothosaurus."

"What exactly is a Nothosaurus?" the doctor wondered.

"Whatever it is, it's a mean son of a bitch." Morgan shook his head. "Crushed my livelihood on wheels like a compacter crushing cardboard."

Daniel glanced over and saw Duncan standing next to them. "Regardless of the damage, we're just lucky to be alive."

"Others not so much," the doctor began. "Six dead that I've seen. Four of them were deputies. One severely injured chief and a terrified mayor and sheriff."

"Daniel's right. We're lucky to be alive," Duncan spoke up. "I have him and Morgan here to thank for that."

"I didn't do anything," Morgan added.

"You kept my kids safe when we were trying to get my wife out. I count that as a good Samaritan move if I ever called one," Duncan smiled. "As well as a damn good review on all the social platforms."

"Thank you but I'm afraid my touring days are over. Got no van to drive them tourists around, see," Morgan chuckled.

"Damn shame that happened." Duncan lowered his head but then shot back up. "Guess you're in the market for a new one then, huh?"

"I couldn't possibly," Morgan started.

"Nonsense! My treat! I own a car dealership in New Hampshire. I'll set you up. Free of charge!"

"I didn't picture you for a car salesman," Daniel chuckled.

"That's how I make the big bucks!" he laughed heartedly.

Anthony looked around. "I think there are more pressing matters at hand. No offense."

"None taken." Duncan smiled and then patted both Daniel and Morgan on the back. He then handed Morgan his business card and told him to call him when he had free time. Afterwards, he returned to his kids, got in the Uber, and went off to the hospital.

"So what do we do about this creature? I mean it can be killed, right?" Morgan wondered.

"Of course it can. However, I think I know of someone who may be able to help," Daniel stated. "Do you know Kane Grant?"

"Sure do," Anthony said. "He works over at Farm Pond." He paused. "In fact, I think that's him over there helping the sheriff now."

Anthony pointed to an older gentleman who seemed athletic for his age. He had a spry, almost chipper stride as he made his way towards some of the victims of the scene that had unfolded less than an hour before. He was chatting with them, placing his hand on shoulders and attempting to calm the frazzled reactions of the witnesses. Daniel wasted no time and hurried over to him.

"Kane Grant."

"Yes?" His voice was raspier than expected.

"Can I talk with you?"

The man looked to the young couple who were still shaken with the horror they had seen. "I'll return with something to drink."

Daniel then guided him away from the distressed duo.

"What can you tell me about the Nothosaurus?"

"The Nothosaurus?" Kane raised an eyebrow.

"The creature that just attacked here. Were there any characteristics about it that you noticed?"

"Characteristics? Um, yeah. It's big, scaly, and pissed off."

"I'm serious."

"Look, Mister. All I can tell you is that I hunted that thing for about a mile and every time I thought I got close enough, it was already two steps ahead. It's fast and cunning, unlike any creature I've ever seen," Kane continued. "I find it awfully convenient that ol' Vanessa is out of her long sleep. Must be that construction they were doing over by Farm Pond."

"Isn't Farm Pond a park?"

"Yes but, on the outskirts, Mayor Owen decided to add some actual farms to a place called Farm Pond. He did that with me and Keith because we're always there. Now he wants to add more. I don't know why. It's mostly brackish ponds. I'm surprised our houses didn't sink into the mud yet. A waste of time and money if you ask me."

"Who's Vanessa?"

"People claim she's a local legend, a myth. She's some serpent-like creature that comes out every so often. I know better," Kane added.

Daniel nodded. "Where's the mayor now?"

"He's probably back at his office, crouching in the corner, nursing a bottle of the cheapest shit he can find."

***

Bill was indeed in his office, but he was not cowering in fear. Rather, he had a plan forming in his mind that needed time to hash out. All the supplies needed would take a few hours to get but he knew he could solve this problem. With or without Vernon's involvement. He would be victorious, solving the problem firsthand. All he needed now was Cortez's chopper and a health supply of firepower.

He had called up Cortez twenty minutes ago and relayed what he needed and when. All that Cortez asked was what they were hunting. Bill had been vague by saying some big fish. More than vague, it was a flat out lie. He did not like the sound of *reptile* and figured Cortez would not metaphorically take the bait. The only thing Cortez offered was some advice. It was not to hook the bastard and to make sure it breached the surface while firing. Bill had asked why, and Cortez told him bullets were slower underwater.

After the call, Bill put some cash into a burlap sack and walked out of the office. Driving down to the hangar, Cortez's words had stuck with him. He decided to stop down by the harbor to get some chum premade and ready to go.

It was a shock to see Burt Groves in one of the slicks. He was sitting on the transom of his fishing vessel. Bill approached apprehensively.

"Groves," Bill said.

The fisherman barely acknowledged him. He seemed lost in thought.

"I could use your help," Bill added.

"Get lost."

"I don't need you, per say. I just need some chum. I'll pay you handsomely for it."

"I said get lost. That means get out of here."

"I know you tried to warn us."

"Even I did not know what we were up against."

"No one could have predicted," Bill began.

"Someone should've! Things have been wrong along this coastline for a while now. Something was off. It wasn't just some random crocodile."

"No one could have predicted a giant dinosaur was going to attack."

"No one saw it until now?" Burt wondered.

Bill stalled to answer.

Burt looked to him. "Did someone know?"

"Kane knew!" another voice came from the boat in the slick behind Bill.

Wilton spoke up. "I heard him when he was first brought in. I may have been drunk but I was lucid enough to hear him ranting and raving about that creature he chased for over a mile."

"… And you locked him away?" Burt chuckled and shook his head. "A lot of this could have been prevented."

"I didn't lock him away. Vernon and his officers did!"

"I'm sure they informed you, hence why you were too tongue tied to say anything just now."

Again, Bill remained silent.

"What's yer plan?" Burt asked.

"My plan is my own. I just need some chum," Bill said flatly.

He then dug out his wallet. "I'll give you a hundred bucks for a bucket of chum with a lid."

"Why, you afraid yer gonna spill it on your suit?"

"Not exactly."

"Two hundred. Chum ain't cheap."

"Isn't that shit just small stuff you catch?"

"Catchin' ain't cheap these days neither."

Bill reluctantly dug out two Hamilton bills and handed them to Burt who then went below and retrieved the chopped-up goods.

"What's the plan, man?" Wilton asked. This time, he seemed genuinely interested.

"I'm going to have to be at a safe enough advantage so that thing can't get me. Then, I'm going to give it a lead lobotomy."

Wilton scoffed. "Good luck. You're definitely going to need it."

CHAPTER TWENTY-ONE

The beast prowled.

It was not being driven back to a place of sanctuary but, rather, called. An abnormal sense of self preservation for a greater purpose overcame it. The power it held over its territory was great and yet it needed to go back to its home. Enraged, the mighty marine reptile slithered through the waters of Oak Bluff and made its way down along the coastline near Seaview Avenue. It soon surfaced as it found its path back home.

She felt weighted down slightly after her high amounts of consumption. Walking along the grassy area, it was hampered by its own excess girth. To any onlookers, the once feared creature looked like a dog who had been fed too much McDonalds. The once slithering serpentine movements it was able to achieve were slowly turning into a fading memory. It was near some familiar bushes that it hunkered down, curling into as small a ball as it could. The dog whimpering in the background was like music to its ears.

Still deadly. Still feared.

***

Anthony Butler pulled into his driveway with a tired expression. It was not even mid-afternoon and already the island was wearing down on him with the creature still being on the loose. There was no knowledge of where it had gone or why it was here, now. Part of him wanted to go back to the hospital and he would. He just needed time to readjust. He was not only mentally fatigued but physically as several nurses had pointed out.

Climbing out of his vehicle, he made his way inside and straight for the kitchen. There was a stillness in the air but he paid it no mind. All he could do was reach for the fridge door and pull out a milk carton. He then poured a glass and enjoyed his refreshment. It went down cool and smoothly like a shot of tequila. That's when the idea entered his frayed mind.

As he entered the downstairs den, he noticed that his pet Pitbull that he was not spending enough time with was not outside of his kennel eager to see him. He figured he'd pour a glass and head out to visit the miserable mutt. Opening the liquor cabinet, he couldn't find any tequila but did see some fireball whiskey. He fished it out and poured a shot glass full. He took a swig and relaxed. It had a slow effect on his numbing mind as far as he could tell.

"Maybe one more," he told himself.

He greedily poured it to the top, spilling some on the bristly rug beneath him. Before he could drink his cinnamon beverage, he heard what sounded like a low growl followed by a whimper. The noise caught him off guard and frightened him so much that he dropped his booze and spun around quickly. It sounded like a guitar string from a bass guitar with a whammy stick reverberating the tone. It was almost inaudible, but he was able to distinguish it through the lack of noise on the quiet June afternoon.

"Mother of Mary."

Approaching the glass sliding doors, he began to second guess what he was about to do. *My phone's upstairs. I should call Daniel. Or maybe even the sheriff.*

Then it came again. Louder this time. It was akin to a car engine revving up.

"Butch," he said to himself.

That dog had been neglected by the doctor for too long. He needed to see if he was okay. To know that he was just scared into his doghouse like last time. There was not much time to waste. He pushed the door across and stepped through what felt like a passage between realms. One of safety and the other of uncertainty. There was no turning back as far as he was concerned. He walked with urgency but was still making slow progress from what he could tell. After what felt like half an hour when, in reality, it had only been a minute, he was halfway across the yard. He kept his eyes on the doghouse, not daring to look away for even a second.

A sound came and it was one of relief for Anthony. A whimper, small and insignificant. The canine was alive. He did not sound hurt, more so afraid.

"Butch. Come here, boy."

Butch did not budge. His owner had a familiar face, but he was too frightened to go outside his comfortable home. With trepidation, he moved over slightly.

To Anthony, it seemed that the dog wanted him to come inside with him. To be safe against any outside evil. It was a perplexing thought given that he did not know dogs could be that considerate. *Maybe I'll have to spend some more time with him.*

It was a nice thought, Anthony's last. He never saw the long, scaly tail rise above him. Nor did he feel it clobber him into a mess of blood, and broken bones with just one swing. It struck him like thunder struck an old oak tree, practically splitting him into two halves vertically. The dog did not move. He did not yelp in fear. He knew his place as blood from his owner splattered onto him.

"His car's here," Daniel said as the taxi brought them up to Anthony's property. "I guess it's been a hell of a day for everyone though."

He, Sandra, and Joseph got out and the cab fare was paid. They stared up at the doctor's home as their ride drove away. The three made their way up to the door. Daniel was relieved to find it unlocked. Sandra guided Joseph down the hall to the guest bedroom.

"Do you see him anywhere?" Daniel called out.

"No," his wife replied.

An empty glass next to a milk carton sat on the kitchen counter. Daniel courteously placed the milk back in the fridge and the glass in the sink. When he looked up after washing the dish, he noticed there was a large dark stain on the lawn. Surrounding it were limbs, uncoiled intestines, and the smashed head of Doctor Anthony Butler.

At first, Daniel did not know what to say, how to react. His old friend was dead and had been killed in a most gruesome fashion. He took a step back from the window and then realized that if the doctor had gone outside, the sliding door may still be open. He quickly hurried to the staircase but stopped dead in his tracks.

There, already on the first step, was the Nothosaurus. Its girth was able to fit up the wide opening though it was seemingly trying to be careful where to step, testing each one to see if they could support its weight. Creaking like an old rocking chair, one of its feet broke through the third step. It was growing irritated and impatient now. It then placed its foot higher up and made its way up the fourth and fifth step.

Daniel could practically feel its hot breath now.

"Honey, what is…" Sandra came up next to him and suddenly stopped and let out a shrill scream.

Snapping out of his amazement that this gargantuan monster was actually making its way upstairs, he turned to his wife and screamed, "Get Joseph!"

Joseph was already standing by the doorway to the guestroom. His mom snagged him by the arm and quickly ushered him towards Daniel. They both stopped when the creature's snout was visible. It stood before Daniel, jaws agape.

"Dad!" Jospeh cried.

"Find a window and get the hell out of here!" Daniel ordered them.

Sandra gripped Joseph's arm tight and brought him back into the guestroom. There was a window, but it was small. She tried to open it but the rusty latches proved difficult.

All the while, Daniel kept on trying to get the slow-moving marine reptile to follow him. He would take a few daring steps towards it and slap its snout. While this action irritated it, it still seemed to be turning more towards his family rather than himself.

"Hey! C'mon! Over here!" Daniel took another step towards it.

The creature was almost halfway into the hallway now. It was pointless to hit its side. All Daniel could do now was go outside and pray that his family was still out there. He hurried to the front door and raced outside. Adrenaline was coursing through his veins like a caffeine addict on his third cup in an hour. When he got around back, he noticed they were not there. As he looked around, he heard a smashing sound. The window above him was broken, glass rained down on him. One shard cut his cheek, another tore his shirt and left a mark right above his chest.

When it was safe to look back up, he saw Joseph being nudged outside. Tears streaming down his face, the boy looked positively horrified.

"C'mon, son, you've got this. Be brave!"

"Ow!" Joseph said mid sob.

He looked down at his bloodied hands. A large chunk of glass was in his palm.

"It's alright! We can get it out after! Just jump! I'll catch you!" Daniel shouted, eyes pleading.

"I can't!"

"Hurry, honey," Sandra tried to tell him in a calming voice, but it was rather tense. "I need you to be strong for me. Okay?"

A sudden roar echoed through the house. It made the walls shake and, in turn, the vibration could be felt in the windowpane. Joseph loosened his grip on it and tumbled out. He fell, spiraling, limbs kicking out. Daniel looked for the best way to grab him. It was as if he were being dragged in several different directions. It all happened fast even though it seemed slow. Daniel extended his arms and caught Joseph. They both fell to the ground on the soft grass.

"Are you okay?" Daniel got to his feet immediately and cradled his son.

"I'm coming down!" Sandra called out to her husband.

Daniel sat Joseph against the house and looked up. She was sitting on the windowsill. Glass was undoubtably digging into the skin on her rear. A painful look covered her face.

"You got this!" Daniel told her.

She took a deep breath and nodded just as the creature's jaws opened around her. She leapt forward as they snapped down on empty air. Daniel caught her. He could not believe it at first. He thought she was gone, taken by the teeth. He looked at her.

"You did it."

The Nothosaurus let out a roar not dissimilar to a siren. It backed away from the window.

Joseph ran up to his parents as they embraced.

"Let's get to a neighbor's house and call the sheriff," Daniel explained.

They broke away from each other and stood up.

"What about Butch?" Joseph asked.

"Who?" Daniel asked.

"The dog."

"It hasn't attacked him at all. I'm sure he'll be fine," Daniel told him. "We, on the other hand, need to go. Now!"

Reluctantly, Joseph went with them. He glanced over his shoulder at the doghouse. The canine seemed content now. Almost as if the evil was indeed gone.

CHAPTER TWENTY-TWO

Trapped.

Sheriff Vernon Hackery had been overjoyed by the news of the creature's capture. Even though it was in a most unorthodox way. He had hurried down to the Butler estate along with his last few deputies. Stanley offered to tag along and was now riding shotgun with Kane to the property. Peter Kemp had heard the news over his CB radio and was rushing to beat the other reporters to the scene. Everyone was ready to get a good look at the monster.

By the time Vernon made his way around back, the last bit of debris had come down. The Nothosaurus had broken through the wall and was now on the loose again. Stanley had pointed out some tracks that led into the yard. They led to a third section of gate that had now been smashed through.

"Still think it's heading back to Farm Pond?" Vernon turned to Kane.

"I don't know what this son of a bitch is doing. All I know is that it has to be stopped."

Without warning, a large mass rammed into Vernon. It knocked him down, pinning him to the ground. White teeth flashed before it as hungry eyes bore into his. Then came the tongue lapping. It licked him as if he were a big juicy steak.

"Will someone get this dog off me!" Vernon called out.

Kane managed to get Butch off of Vernon, but he quickly wiggled himself free of his collar and took off into the house.

"What the hell's gotten into that mutt?" Vernon wondered while wiping the slime off his face.

"Doesn't matter. We need to move now before we lose it again!" Kane ordered.

Stanley pointed to the sky. "Uh, I think someone else is already on the move."

Everyone followed his finger just as a chopper came overhead and circled the area. It was clear that they too were hunting the horror that had been terrorizing the island community.

"Who the hell is that?" Vernon asked.

Peter focused his camera on the branding of the helicopter. "It looks like it's Cortez's chopper service. In the cockpit there's…" He stopped.

"Who is in there?" Vernon demanded.

"You're not going to believe it. It's our mayor!"

***

Bill Owen was a very fortunate man. He had found his way into politics after a nearly disastrous event took place. A woman claimed the multi-millionaire had sexually assaulted her. She had some convincing evidence and a witness. It was when the witness was discovered to be the notorious Don the Con that the case was almost thrown out. Don had done everything from form false accusations to launder money to even run a false prostitution syndicate. One where he had acquired attractive women to steal from lonely rich old men.No one knew what Don the Con looked like. They only had a name and what he did. It was slipup that saved Bill's righteous rump. The woman claimed Don the Con had had him perform the dastardly deed, attempting to throw both men under the bus and reap the rewards.

It did not go as planned.

She was fined heavily. Not many people saw her after that. She was the talk of the night circuit for a while. Then, poof, she vanished. Bill had received a random call one afternoon a few years ago. The person on the other end claimed to be the woman's husband and that he would be coming after him. Vernon had had the wire tapped during the second call. It turned out to be an islander who did not like his politics or him as a person.

Don the Con's elusive client was never talked about after that. Now, flying over the Atlantic, Bill began to think about her. He pondered on if she was taken out by one of the petty crook's men for having him put away. Was she tossed into the sea, bound by rope or chain that was tied to a rock? Did the fish like the taste of cold-hearted bitch? He knew it did not matter but the thought still crept through him like a winter chill from a stiff breeze.

"Damn, where the hell is it?" he said aloud.

"What was that?" Cortez's voice came over the headset.

Clearing his voice, Bill spoke into the microphone piece. "I don't think it's out here."

Cortez did not respond. Instead, he seemed to be listening to something or someone on the radio. He nodded and turned to look at Bill over his shoulder.

"There are reports that it's near Anthony Butler's property."

"No," Bill said, coldly.

"Apparently, it made a mess of the doctor. Dog's okay though." Cortez gave a nervous chuckle.

"Take us back that way. Pronto!"

"Roger that."

The Huey made a wide turn and then flew back inland. Soon, Bill was scouring over Nantucket Avenue. There were several cars parked outside the doctor's estate. More began to pull up in a short amount of time. During the horde of interest, Bill thought he noticed something odd. There was a wide clearing made by something. It led towards Farm Pond.

"It's headed for the trail. Damnit! Kane was right!"

"Let's check it out," Cortez said and followed the carved-out path in the grass.

They made it to the trail in less than thirty seconds. The wide body of water seemed to be shallower than normal. The clearness of the surface gave way to a dark patch.

"I think that's where it lives!"

"Why is there a crevasse in the pond?" Cortez wondered.

"It must have been hibernating there. The nearby construction. It must have woken it up!"

"Way ta go, Mayor. Now the only question is, where the fu-"

"Look out!" Bill cried.

Cortez's attention snapped towards a pilot's worst fear. A flock of seagulls were flying directly towards them. Bill grabbed the chum bucket to secure it, preparing for the worst. He needed that bait if he were to stop the creature. Chopping them to bits like a Veggie Masher, chunks of seagull splattered and sprayed all over the helicopter. The framework rattled and the engine puttered. Then, without warning, the helicopter tilted to the left. Bill let go of the chum which rolled out of the cockpit and into the pond below. He needed to find something to grab onto. His hands searched wildly. With one desperate grip, he squeezed the pilot's throat from behind the seat.

"Keep it steady!" Bill screamed.

Reaching for the mayor's hands, he tried to free himself, but it was useless. The man had a grip like a vice. The last thing Cortez thought before slipping unconscious was that the mayor must give one mean handshake.

The helicopter tilted forward as Cortez relinquished the controls.

"Shhhhiiiittt!" Bill screamed.

He had no choice. Either he could take a plunge with the chopper, get chopped up by the blades, or go for a swim. He looked around for a gun but remembered Cortez had them stashed and secured under his seat. There was only one way to fix this and still be able to have a chance to stop the creature.

Letting go, he dove, feet first into the shallow pond. His feet hit bottom within seconds though they did not touch mud. Instead, they pressed against the chum bucket which immediately popped open. Bill almost wanted to laugh underwater. *Of all the places.*

It did not take him long to surface. When he did, he saw the chopper had crashed near the shore. It had not exploded like in the movies. Though that did not mean it wouldn't. He made a break for the chopper. The chum was gone and now he was the bait. His breaststroke would only last so long. He was not as fit as he used to be. Soon though, he reached the chopper. There were no signs of the creature yet. There had not been this whole time. He began to think it would be ironic if it was not even in Farm Pond.

On the verge of laughing, he stopped in his tracks. He heard an expulsion of water spray that jetted out from one's snout. He turned and silently prayed it was a cow or a deer or something. The aircraft was a few feet away. He still had a chance. He did not see the creature but could sense its presence. He gulped nervously as he saw the crocodilian snout no more than five yards out in the eel grass. It was covered in barnacles and had a fierceness in its eyes.

"Stay back!" Bill gave a shrill order.

There was no sign that it understood or feared him. Instead, it kept inching forward.

"Get away."

Still no signs of slowing.

It encroached upon him like a predatory cat cornering its cowering prey. Those eyes were reptilian but also had the intensity of a big feline. They scared Bill Owen. Scared him to his core and rattled his mind.

"Please," he begged to the aquatic reptile. "I just wanted what was best!"

It charged without warning. Five yards became four. Three. Two. One.

Boom!

Several shots rang out. They continuously pelted into the Nothosaurus' face, below its ear, and its side. Blood gushed out in juicy squirts. Every bullet found its mark. The eruption of gore was almost beautiful. The bright crimson plasma began to form a red cloud around the creature. Then, for the final blow, a bullet struck its right eye.

It attempted to dive but was weakened by the onslaught on lead rounds entering its body. It floated to the surface and turned on its back.

Bill turned and saw Vernon, Kane, and Stanley lower their weapons and Peter, his camera.

CHAPTER TWENTY-THREE

Never forgotten.

It was Saturday, June 21st. The Jaws weekend was in full swing and the joy of the marine reptile having been dispatched reached internet and social platforms of all types. Media coverage was circulating fast. It was #1 in trending and would probably be so for some time. Its body had been hauled out of Farm Pond a few hours after the extermination. Peter Kemp had made sure to get plenty of pictures and video of the event. He was going to make it big.

Scientists, paleontologists, marine biologists the world over were being flown in to determine if it were a hoax and, if not, how to proceed. Daniel was at the forefront when it came time for the autopsy. After all, his family had been put through the ringer twice.

The Nothosaurus nearly doubled the tourism and revenue. It was the Jaws of the twenty-first century. A sense of pride came from Martha's Vineyard and its citizens. It was not like it had been right after the film was released where people felt their lives were being invaded and interrupted continuously. It was just round two but, this time, they were more prepared.

Before the bigwigs of the science world were to arrive, Daniel arranged a special meeting with Kane Grant. The two sat in the mayor's office while Bill went to Espresso Love for a cup of joe.

"You were right all along," Daniel stated.

"Me and Keith were right. That damn thing killed him. It killed so many."

"You should have been believed. Much like a lot of these scenarios, you have to take spoken word with a grain of salt. Especially these days," Daniel explained.

"Well. Regardless. You've got your corpse. I just have one question. How and why was it living in Farm's Pond?"

"I hope the autopsy will give us more details on that."

Kane nodded. "Bill said something about a crater in the pond?"

"A crevasse. We presume it was hibernating there. I don't know how it lasted so long. It must have been old given the fact that rifles took it down."

"She."

"She?"

"Yep. She. I know a bitch when I see one."

Daniel sat silently for a moment. "We'll know more once the autopsy is completed."

"In the meantime, I take it I can get back to work?"

"Just don't drink on the job."

"That was Keith. Most of the time." Kane's voice trailed off.

"A word of advice. If you want people to take you seriously now, drop the bottle."

It was Kane's turn to nod and sit there quietly.

Eventually, the two men stood up and walked out of the office.

"Thank you for everything, Mr. Grant."

"I want to be there," Kane said as Daniel placed his hand on the door handle.

"What?"

"I want to be there. Whether it's in the operating room or behind some observation glass. I want to be there when the autopsy's performed."

"I'll see what strings I can pull. It's already going to be a tight fit. Even for me."

Kane pushed past Daniel and continued down the hallway. He passed Bill who tried to wave him goodbye but didn't want to spill his coffee.

***

Morgan had just finished his second tour and was now heading home. He was feeling overjoyed by the amount of income he received compared to other guides. He had witnessed the Nothosaurus firsthand and lived. He had plenty to tell and many wanted to listen. He would grant them that opportunity for the right price.

He passed by a restaurant and saw Stanley chatting up some waitress who seemed to be fawning over him. Morgan chuckled.

"Live it up, kid."

He thought about it and decided maybe he should dip his toes back into the dating circle. He was not terribly old and knew his way around a conversation. The guilt he felt for those kids being eaten still ate at him and he did not want to dump that burden on anyone else. He would have to think about it long and hard.

As he drove past Jaws bridge, he did not bother looking at it. He had a hard enough time, it being a tourist hotspot that his clientele desperately wanted to visit. He was going to have to find himself first. A new sense of comfort. In the meantime, as the sun began to set beyond the horizon and the water turned a blackish blue, he began to mumble a tune.

Da nun. Da nun. Da nun.

Check out other great

Sea Monster Novels!

Michael Cole

SCAR

Scar is a killing machine. Born from DNA spliced between the extinct Megalodon and modern day Great White, he has a viciousness that transcends time. His evil is reflected in his eyes, his savagery in his two-inch serrated teeth, his ruthlessness in his trail of death. After escaping captivity, the killer shark travels to the island community Cross Point, where prey is in abundance. With an insatiable appetite, heightened senses, and skin impervious to bullets, Scar kills everything that crosses his path. His reign of terror puts him at war with the island sheriff, Nick Piatt. With the body count rising, Nick vows to protect his island community from the vicious threat. With the aid of a marine biologist, a rookie deputy, and a bad-tempered fisherman, Nick leads a crusade against Scar, as well as the ruthless scientist who created him.

Rick Chesler

HOTEL MEGALODON

An underwater luxury hotel on a gorgeous tropical island is set for an extravagant opening weekend with the world watching. The only thing standing in the way of a first-rate experience for the jet-setting VIPs is an unscrupulous businessman and sixty feet of prehistoric shark. As the underwater complex is besieged by a marauding behemoth, newly minted marine biologist Coco Keahi must face off against the ancient predator as it rises from the deep with a vengeance. Meanwhile, a human monster has decided he would be better off if Coco were one of the creature's victims.

Check out other great

Sea Monster Novels!

Michael Cole

CREATURE OF LAKE SHADOW

It was supposed to be a simple bank robbery. Quick. Clean. Efficient. It was none of those. With police searching for them across the state, a band of criminals hide out in a desolate cabin on the frozen shore of Lake Shadow. Isolated, shrouded in thick forest, and haunted by a mysterious history, they thought it was the perfect place to hide. Tensions mount as they hear strange noises outside. Slain animals are found in the snow. Before long, they realize something is watching them. Something hungry, violent, and not of this world. In their attempt to escape, they found the Creature of Lake Shadow.

C.J. Waller

PREDATOR X

When deep level oil fracking uncovers a vast subterranean sea, a crack team of cavers and scientists are sent down to investigate. Upon their arrival, they disappear without a trace. A second team, including sedimentologist Dr Megan Stoker, are ordered to seek out Alpha Team and report back their findings. But Alpha team are nowhere to be found – instead, they are faced with something unexpected in the depths. Something ancient. Something huge. Something dangerous. Predator X

Check out other great

Sea Monster Novels!

Matt James

SUB-ZERO

The only thing colder than the Antarctic air is the icy chill of death... Off the coast of McMurdo Station, in the frigid waters of the Southern Ocean, a new species of Antarctic octopus is unintentionally discovered. Specialists aboard a state-of-the-art DARPA research vessel aim to apply the animal's "sub-zero venom" to one of their projects: An experimental painkiller designed for soldiers on the front lines. All is going according to plan until the ship is caught in an intense storm. The retrofitted tanker is rocked, and the onboard laboratory is destroyed. Amid the chaos, the lead scientist is infected by a strange virus while conducting the specimen's dissection. The scientist didn't die in the accident. He changed.

Alister Hodge

THE CAVERN

When a sink hole opens up near the Australian outback town of Pintalba, it uncovers a pristine cave system. Sam joins an expedition to explore the subterranean passages as paramedic support, hoping to remain unneeded at base camp. But, when one of the cavers is injured, he must overcome paralysing claustrophobia to dive pitch-black waters and squeeze through the bowels of the earth. Soon he will find there are fates worse than being buried alive, for in the abandoned mines and caves beneath Pintalba, there are ravenous teeth in the dark. As a savage predator targets the group with hideous ferocity, Sam and his friends must fight for their lives if they are ever to see the sun again.

www.ingramcontent.com/pod-product-compliance
Lightning Source LLC
Chambersburg PA
CBHW061240170626
46809CB00007B/2752

* 9 7 8 1 9 2 3 1 6 5 6 5 6 *